"About that k   said.

"I kissed Matt, not y   Santa costume."

"No. You kissed me in the Santa costume. And I think you already know it."

"In your dreams."

"Really? Then why are you always staring at me?"

"I'm not always staring at you!"

When Bryan only waited patiently, she blew out a frustrated breath. "Much," she muttered.

"I'm flattered," he said.

"Don't be! I did not kiss you!"

"I could prove it to you, if you like."

He could prove it to her. Oh, Lord. Katie's palms were clammy, her heart raced. The flu, she decided. But that didn't explain why the thought of him "proving it" to her had her nipples hard and achy. "How could you prove something that never happened?" she asked with remarkable—totally false—calm.

"By kissing you again…"

Dear Reader

Ever kiss that perfect guy? In KISS ME, KATIE! my heroine thinks she has. Only problem, she laid her lips on the wrong guy, and now that wrong guy—the baddest, sexiest man in town, thank you very much—wants another kiss! And who can resist Bryan Morgan? Because once the daredevil rebel has his mind set on something he gets it, and he most definitely has his mind set on Katie.

Happy holidays,

Jill Shalvis

KISS ME, KATIE!

BY
JILL SHALVIS

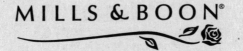

MILLS & BOON®

MILLS & BOON and MILLS & BOON with the Rose Device are registered trademarks of the publisher.

First published in Great Britain 2002
Harlequin Mills & Boon Limited,
Eton House, 18-24 Paradise Road, Richmond, Surrey TW9 1SR

© Jill Shalvis 2000

ISBN 0 263 82991 X

Set in Times Roman 10½ on 13 pt.
01-1202-32274

Printed and bound in Spain
by Litografia Rosés, S.A., Barcelona

1

SHE WAS REALLY going to do it, she was going to seduce Santa Claus. It wasn't that she had a thing for guys in a white beard and red suit, although she did have to admit, she liked the belly laugh.

But what Katie Wilkins really wanted was the man beneath the costume. Mr. Perfect from the executive offices down the hall. He was everything she wanted in a man: mature, polished...safe. So safe that she'd known him all year and he hadn't once made a move on her.

She hoped to change that tonight.

The holiday party was in full swing around her, even though Christmas was still three weeks away. Christmas carols blared out of speakers hanging from the rafters of the hangar, and everyone from the airplane mechanics to Mr. Riggs, the director of Wells Aircraft—the small, private airport where they all worked—was ready to party with the proper festive spirit.

The spiked punch helped.

Or that's what Katie figured when she saw Mrs. Giddeon, their usually prim receptionist, with an empty glass in one hand and Mr. Riggs in the other, a decisively naughty gleam in her eye as she dragged him toward the mistletoe hanging from the nose of a jet parked in the far corner.

Then there were Dale, Jake and Evan, the linemen, and usually the most polite of young men, cheering and egging on Julie, Cassandra and Eloise, three of the women in her office, who were at the moment exhibiting go-go dancing skills to the tune of "Jingle Bell Rock."

Katie shook her head in amazement. She hadn't imagined this when she'd volunteered to decorate. She'd known everyone had been working hard, trying to keep up with the expansion plans that had them putting in long hours and stressful times with new clients. But to totally let loose? Was she the only grown-up here?

It felt like it.

And yet, from deep inside her came a yearning to join them, to brush off years of restraint, down a glass of spiked punch and toss caution to the wind.

Which brought her back to jumping Santa's bones.

Katie glanced across the huge hangar, wildly

decorated with gold and silver streamers, red and green ornaments, and of course the pathetic four-foot Christmas tree. Pathetic because, this being Southern California, and a drought year at that, the poor tree looked as though it were on its last legs.

Next to the straining tree stood Santa. Tall, smiling and charismatic. Because she knew who was under the suit, Matt Osborne, a.k.a. Mr. Perfect, her heart sighed.

Go for it, a little voice whispered in her head. *Do it. Kiss him.*

As a rule, Katie didn't feel the holiday spirit. She wasn't exactly Scrooge, but the truth was, she'd been Christmas cursed. It had all started when she was six. Her neighbor, Holly Stone, got the Barbie vacation house and Katie didn't. Then, when they were twelve, and still neighbors, Holly cheated at her holiday party spin-the-bottle game in order to kiss the boy Katie had a crush on. The topper had come three years ago, when they'd been twenty-one—no longer neighbors, but in the small town of San Limo there was no escaping anyone—and Holly had stolen Katie's fiancé.

Her own fault really. Katie knew she was too careful, too methodical…too much like an accountant, darn it. Yes, she was happy enough, financially stable, yadda yadda.

But she was also dateless.

This was the year that would change. No more bad luck. She was going to see to it herself. She was going to make a Christmas wish, a really good one, and make sure it came true.

What she would wish for would be different from anything she'd ever wished for before. Not a new adding machine, not a new pair of slippers, not a new set of I.R.S. regulations. No, this year she wanted a knockout kiss from Matt Osborne; sophisticated, handsome, intelligent, and all-around perfect guy.

"You're not going to chicken out, are you?"

Katie rolled her eyes, then because that was an irrationally childish gesture, she carefully schooled her features into indifference before turning to face Holly, aforementioned arch rival, and unfortunate co-worker. Holly was decked out in a sexy little silver-sequined number that blared self-confidence, and a perfect size-six frame, to the world.

"I never chicken out," Katie said.

Holly laughed deeply. "We don't have time to go down that road."

"I don't see *you* kissing anyone."

"I'm not the one with a boring sex life."

Nonexistent was more like it, Katie thought.

"Besides…" Holly examined her perfect manicure, which was neon red and topped with ten different, and very wicked, appliqués of Santa in compromising situations. "If *I* wanted to kiss Matt, I'd just go right up to him, grab him and plant one on him. I'm not shy."

No kidding. Katie had plenty of incidents to prove that one, years' and years' worth, but time was passing and she had a mission—getting Santa beneath the mistletoe, mistletoe she'd purposely planted in several spots with grand hopes for the evening ahead.

In light of that, Katie squinted across the action-filled hangar, past the confetti-covered Cessnas and Learjets and overdressed office staff, to the man in the red suit. "You sure Matt is the one in there?"

They both studied Santa. He had a red festive hat, a white beard and mustache. He also wore the required stuffed belly and red suit. He looked... jolly. But that could have been caused by the very spiked punch. Truthfully, other than being the correct height, which was approximately six feet tall, there was absolutely no way to be certain *who* was under there.

"It's him," Holly said decisively.

Katie definitely knew better than to trust her, but what could go wrong this time? Everyone knew

Matt was going to be Santa, it'd been in the weekly office memo.

The office memo never lied.

"Okay." She handed her still full flute to Holly. "Wish me luck."

"Merry Kissing and Happy Fondling," Holly said, lifting her drink in a toast.

Katie smoothed her dress in a useless attempt to scoot the thing farther down on her thighs. Purchasing the bold, red, stretchy number had been a huge departure for her, not to mention a bit of a strain on her checkbook. She could only hope Santa liked it, since she'd spent nearly her entire month's budget on it.

That was okay. If it worked, it'd be well worth having to eat macaroni and cheese from a box for the next month.

She stopped tugging at the hem and straightened, which emphasized the provocative bodice. *Good.* She, secret chicken of the world, needed all the help she could get. With a hard swallow, she let her high heels lead the way.

To Santa.

To the perfect man beneath the costume.

To a good, hot Christmas kiss.

He saw her coming, she watched as he focused

in on her. To be sure he got the full effect, she took a deep breath.

In response, Santa...choked on his drink. The woman standing next to him, Edwina, who ran the small coffee shop in the lobby, starting pounding on his back, which brought on a fresh attack of coughing.

Grabbing his glass, Edwina set it aside and lifted his arms over his head—or that's what she tried to do, but as Santa was tall and Edwina was...well, not, the only thing she managed to accomplish was to flail his arms near the region of his chest as she bounced up and down in front of him.

From a distance, this seemed like some sort of comical dance, and since Edwina wore a short green cocktail dress, now flapping wildly as she leaped around in front of him, she looked like an elf to Matt's Santa.

Finally, he waved a hand to indicate he was fine, and when he managed to convince Edwina of this, she left him alone.

"I think it's the costume," she whispered as she passed Katie. "It's really such a trial to wear it successfully. That poor man should be nominated for sainthood."

"I agree," Katie murmured, because now that she was close, she could see how right Edwina was.

The suit had to weigh a ton, what with the heavy red material and white faux fur, not to mention the added belly and big black boots.

Could she even press close enough past all that tummy to kiss him?

Yes, she decided. Yes, she could. Besides, she couldn't back out now, not with Holly's gaze burning a mocking, laughing hole in her back.

The mistletoe she'd decided on was only about five feet behind Matt, around the corner, out of view from the rest of the party. Smiling sweetly, heart thundering, she stepped closer. She really didn't know what she expected…maybe for him to make things easy, to back up, possibly right beneath the hanging plant?

He didn't. Instead, he held his ground, watching her from beneath the silliest pair of glasses she'd ever seen. The outside of the lenses were tinted in a design of Santa's bright, laughing eyes, so that she couldn't see Matt's own blue gaze.

She assumed he was smiling, too. Hard to tell with the beard, but hoping for the best, she took another step, silently willing him to help her out.

Why wasn't he backing up?

Instead he tilted his head, as if asking her what she was doing.

She thought that should be rather obvious!

"I don't know if you realize this," she said. "But right behind you and around the corner, there's some mistletoe...just sort of hanging there."

Nothing.

"I helped decorate. It's waiting for some couple to get themselves beneath it. So they can kiss," she added helpfully.

Still no response!

Okay, she could admit she didn't know Matt well, but she did know he wasn't an idiot. He was vice president, for God's sake. Yes, he was sedate, he was mature and focused, but she was offering to kiss him!

What was wrong with him? According to *Cosmopolitan* magazine, there wasn't a red-blooded man alive who would turn down a kiss! The editors had promised!

But Matt didn't budge and her nerve was fading fast. She was beginning to feel very sorry she'd ever thought about doing this. In fact, maybe she should switch her Christmas wish from a kiss to a big black hole opening up in the floor so it could swallow her.

"You *are* in there, aren't you?" she asked with a teasing smile to hide her embarrassment.

Slowly Santa turned and craned his neck, study-ing the plant in question.

Then looked back at her.

She smiled encouragingly, knowing her time was running out. Any second now, Holly was going to decide she wanted Matt for herself, and she'd have no such difficulties getting him—or any man—beneath that blasted mistletoe.

No, she couldn't fail. Take charge time.

Grabbing Santa's hand, she pulled him around the corner, noting his hand was big and warm and callused. At the first tug she also took in the fact that he seemed bigger and more powerful than Matt's lean physique had led her to believe, but now wasn't the time to dwell on that when she had him so close to her goal.

The noise of the party followed them, but they were completely alone in the hallway. Around them, all the office doors were shut, with not an-other soul in sight. The music and laughter from the party seemed almost surreal.

They were in their own little world.

Right beneath the mistletoe.

And he was staring at her from behind those ri-diculous glasses and fake facial hair; the only real part of him available to her was his mouth.

Perfect, since that was all she happened to need at the moment.

Reaching up to touch his shoulders, she leaned in close. "Merry Christmas, Matt," she whispered, and set her lips to his in the connection she'd been dreaming about all night.

She felt his startled jerk, felt the immediate tensing of his big body, but she just pressed closer and deepened the kiss, swallowing the growl of desire he made.

Of course it also could have been a sound of surprise, since she'd given him little choice in this kissing matter, but she figured if he hated it, he'd back off.

He didn't.

Instead, his hands went to her waist, tightening when she pulled off his glasses and tossed them over his shoulder. He tasted like champagne...like wonderful, delicious male...like *heaven*. It was better than her wildest dreams, and then he was tilting her head for better access and kissing her back. She nearly fell to the floor because it was the most blazingly, most pleasurable sensation she'd ever experienced in her life.

One of his large hands cupped her cheek, his fingers playing havoc over her skin as he slowly pulled back and stared at her.

She nearly staggered from the wonder of it all. Never had a kiss so rocked her world, left her so off balance, so dizzy with rocketing emotions. "That…was some mistletoe," she gasped.

"It had nothing to do with the mistletoe."

No, he was right, she could see that in his blue eyes, in the lines of his mouth, that wonderful, soft yet firm, incredibly talented, mouth.

Confusion had her taking a step back, so that Santa's hands fell to his sides. This was supposed to be just a kiss, she thought, not a life altering moment with the emotional impact of an 8.0 earthquake. "Gotta go," she managed to murmur.

Yeah, she definitely had to go. Maybe she really *was* just a chicken, but Lord have mercy, how could she have known what would happen to her insides over one silly embrace? It made her feel things; wild, reckless, *hot* things that she'd never felt before.

Had never wanted to feel. All she'd wanted was one kiss! A silly little Christmas wish. But she'd gotten much more.

"Katie."

She heard him call her name, in a voice made so thick by desire that she didn't recognize it, but she kept moving, had to keep moving.

Wow. Just wow.

Because she needed a moment to herself, she escaped into one of the darkened offices. It took more than a few deep breaths to calm her racing heart and throbbing body. It took a while longer before she realized she'd gotten far more than she'd bargained for.

By the time she reentered the party, Matt stood by the tree, the Santa costume gone. How did he get rid of it so fast? And why? When she caught his eye, she could only stare, still amazed by the connection they'd shared.

"Good evening." His voice was perfectly calm. Almost asleep calm.

Catatonic calm.

"It looks as though nearly everyone showed up tonight," he said.

How could he sound so…so *normal?* With one kiss he'd leveled her, and yet he stood there as if it'd been no big deal.

Was it possible he hadn't felt what she had?

And how humiliating was *that?*

"Matt, about what just happened—"

He looked at her blankly. "What just happened?"

"Exactly," she said, nodding. "About that—"

"Excuse me?"

''No, excuse *me*,'' came a low, husky male voice that made Katie's entire body tighten.

Bryan Morgan.

Head pilot and local daredevil. He was the hero of every man at Wells Aviation, and the center of every woman's fantasy.

Every woman but Katie. He was a jump-off-the-cliff type of guy, far too similar to her daredevil father who had gotten himself killed when she was just a teenager. As a rule she steered clear of him, though the reasons were so complicated she didn't often allow herself to think about them.

Especially now, when he was smiling at her, a wide, devastatingly charismatic smile that would have melted any other female in the room.

''You look lovely,'' he said, which was funny only because he was tall, leanly muscled, rugged, and the most gorgeous man ever to walk the planet, and *he* thought *she,* plain-Jane Katie, looked lovely. Right.

''Thank you,'' she said politely, pointedly turning away from him back to Matt. Darn it, she wanted to talk about their kiss.

''And the decorations,'' Bryan said, a small smile in his voice. ''So tastefully done.''

Great. He liked the decorations. Now could he just go away? She had a kiss to discuss!

"Especially all that strategically placed mistletoe," Bryan added, and Katie finally went still, giving him her one-hundred-percent undivided attention.

"What?" she whispered, her heart all but stopping.

Bryan just looked at her, his brilliant blue eyes innocent. And hot. Now she realized that was a complete contradiction, but it happened to be true. Something deep down within her unfurled, hesitated. "What did you just say?" she asked again.

He merely smiled. "Nothing. Nothing at all."

2

BRYAN MORGAN threw his plane into a spin, acknowledging he had about ten seconds to pull himself out if he wanted to live.

Nine…eight…

The image of last night's party floated through the haze in his mind. There'd been plenty of loud talking and even louder music, reminding him of his huge family. Growing up with six older sisters, there hadn't been a lot of quiet, or alone time. So he had a fine appreciation of both. Because of that, he liked his parties a lot more intimate and personal…but there had been one redeeming factor last night. A surprising one.

A woman. Now, Bryan loved women, he really did. All shapes and sizes. But in his mind, he already had a permanent force of at least seven in his life, if he counted his mother as well as his sisters. All of whom had bossed, charmed, coaxed and threatened their way for each of his thirty-two years. And since they showed signs of living another half a century at least, it wasn't often Bryan allowed another woman to play a serious role in his existence.

In fact, it was downright rare. Oh, he dated. Often. But things were always on a walk-away basis.

Always.

And yet last night he'd held Katie and his heart had sort of fumbled. Warm, vital, sweet, funny Katie, with her soft, wavy, whiskey-colored hair that matched her whiskey-colored eyes, eyes in the past that had always looked at him so aloofly.

Seven...six...

She'd looked amazing in that shimmery red dress. Who would have thought? He'd even dreamed of it, the way it had fallen over her curvy little body and trim thighs. So different from her usual prim-and-proper business attire, which suited her accounting position, but not the heat and passion he knew lurked just beneath her surface.

Well, to be fair, he didn't know for *certain* she had heat and passion beneath her surface, he'd known her all year and hadn't been able to tell... until last night.

In spite of the force of gravity pulling his face into a grimace, he managed a grin. Because now he knew, oh yeah, he definitely knew.

Five...four... But what he *didn't* know was why

she seemed so wary of him. Over the years he'd caused a lot of feelings in women, most of them pretty good, some of them not so good, but never once had he caused wariness.

Three…and the plane continued to spin. So did his head, bringing his thoughts back to the task at hand.

Now was not the time to be daydreaming about things that would drain the rest of the blood from his head to parts south.

He needed his wits.

He was good at flying, really good, and it wasn't cockiness that told him that, but fact. Yes, he was confident, but then again, a good pilot had to be, and Bryan was nothing if not a good pilot.

Two… He hoped they were getting the shot they needed below, that the cameras hadn't failed as they had earlier because he really didn't think he could pull off this particular stunt any better than he just had.

It was the perfect ride, glorious blue skies, not a cloud in sight and…

One. Just a flash second before hurtling both him and a very expensive plane into the ground, he pulled out of the spin and shook his head slightly to clear it.

''Got it?'' he asked into his headset.

"Holy cow!" Ritchie yelled into Bryan's ear. "*Holy, ace,* that was absolutely amazing!"

"Gee, guess you got it."

"You're wasting your talents taxiing the rich and famous in expensive airplanes, you should be doing stunts *all* the time."

Ritchie Owens was a Hollywood producer. That's what he told women, anyway. Mostly he did beer commercials. The stunt Bryan had just pulled off would be shown in an adventurous, exciting, quick-paced, filled with loud music ad spot designed to raise a man's thirst.

Or so he supposed.

Bryan didn't really care; it gave him an excuse to fly, and to fly with abandon, and that was all that mattered to him. "I don't taxi people. I run a charter company."

"Yeah, yeah, whatever. Still a waste."

Bryan didn't bother to correct Ritchie. He didn't feel any particular need to defend himself, not when he truly did love his work. In his opinion, he had everything he would ever need, and Ritchie, all four and a half feet of him, driven by the materialistic meter of success of the film industry, would never understand.

"God, that was fantastic." Ritchie was clearly ecstatic. "The best I've ever seen! We're gonna get tons of feedback from this one, ace. *Tons.* I feel it in my bones.''

Bryan remained silent as he easily circled and came in for his landing. The sun was at his back, the wind was with him. On top of the world, he took a deep breath, as always awed by the glory of being in the air.

No problems, no stress. Life was everything he wanted, everything he made out of it.

But inexplicably, that wasn't the case today. And if he was being honest, something he always was to a fault—just ask any of his past girlfriends—he had to admit it had everything to do with last night.

The Christmas party.

And the surprise Christmas kiss.

It'd been a helluva great gift. Admittedly, the gift giver hadn't meant to give *him* the kiss, but he'd tried to tell her he wasn't who she thought he was, hadn't he?

Well…maybe he hadn't tried very hard.

Maybe he hadn't managed to say anything except her name, but he was only human. And yeah, maybe a better man might have told her the truth right then and there, but he wasn't out for any hero awards.

He just wanted the girl.

He'd been momentarily stunned into meathead

status when Katie had touched her warm lips to his, not to mention dizzy as hell from those stupid Santa glasses he'd been wearing.

He still had a headache from them.

And anyway, what was a woman doing even *thinking* of kissing a guy as boring and predictable as Matt Osborne? It was a crime, in his humble opinion, a total crime.

Bryan completed his landing without incident, tied the plane down on his own even though there was a staff of linemen waiting to assist as there always was, and also a film crew who'd paid to use the tarmac for the morning. He tipped his head to stare at the sky.

"Already yearning to be back up there?"

He recognized the female voice and braced himself.

"We have a great staff, you know." Holly, who'd come up behind him, managed to casually brush her long, lithe, very toned body against his. "Why do you always insist on doing everything yourself?"

Seemed silly to tell her the truth, when she didn't care about the truth. What she cared about, what she'd cared about for the entire two weeks since she'd come to this place as the new office manager, was getting action.

Man action.

Apparently he was the man.

"Do you do all your own handling because you like to sweat?" Holly wondered, circling him until she was in front of him, smiling with all the innocence of a shark. "Or because you like the way all us silly females melt over you when you do?"

"Oh, definitely, it's because I like to sweat."

She laughed softly. "So big and tough."

"You should see me after I wash the plane."

His light sarcasm was a wasted effort. She merely smiled. "You're so exciting, Bryan. How did you manage to keep all those tipsy women off you last night? It wouldn't have anything to do with the...Santa costume?"

"I thought my being Santa was a secret."

Holly arched a brow and let out a mysterious smile. "Whoever told you that?"

"You know who. *You.* I got your note that Matt would be late and couldn't do it, so you needed *me* to do it, and to keep it quiet about it."

"Oh, *that* note." She purred and lowered her lashes. "I suppose I owe you now."

Oh, boy. "No. Consider that a freebie." Besides, he'd gotten his reward.

"A freebie?" Holly pursed her lips. "You wouldn't, by any chance, have gotten...*lucky* with that costume last night, would you? Maybe lucky with a certain accountant who thought you were…oh, I don't know, a certain vice president?''

Ah, now it made sense. He'd been set up. ''You were responsible for that?''

''You're giving me far too much credit,'' she said serenely, studying her manicure. ''And besides, everyone knows, Matt was supposed to be Santa.''

''Yes,'' he said patiently. ''But Matt *wasn't* Santa. I was.''

''Right. So if a mistake was made—'' she lifted her shoulders and sent him a guileless smile ''—then…oops.''

''You told her Matt was in the costume, didn't you?''

''Not exactly.''

''Then what, exactly?''

''Are you telling me you didn't enjoy that kiss?''

''Okay, let's do this another way. Does she or does she not *now* know the truth?''

''Not.'' Holly grinned. ''Are you kidding? Prim-and-proper accounting Katie kissing the wild, reckless, rowdy, untamable Bryan Morgan? She'd have a coronary. She definitely doesn't like guys like you.''

''She's not all *that* prim and proper.''

Holly bent at the waist and burst out laughing. "Do tell."

Bryan gave up and started walking toward the first of three hangars that made up Wells, knowing he had exactly one hour to take care of his paperwork before chartering a flight that would keep him out of the airport for the rest of the day.

Without a doubt, he was going to have to put that kiss right out of his head. Yes, the little accountant kissed nice, so what? She didn't like guys like him, so what? He didn't care, not when there were plenty of other women in the sea.

That he hadn't been looking was another matter entirely, he told himself. Between work and his loving but demanding family, he'd been busy, and hadn't needed the additional complication. And he knew all too well, women were definitely a complication, no matter how sweet yet sexy their light, expressive whiskey eyes were.

With that in mind, he made it to the hallway outside the postage-stamp-size office he rented from Wells, when he heard a very familiar voice.

"Matt? Matt, I know you're in there."

Katie.

Katie back in her dull business suit with the too long skirt and the too full blazer so he couldn't so much as catch a glimpse of that lush body he now knew she had, knocking on the closed door of Matt Osborne's office.

She should look unappealing, but she didn't, not at all. Instead, she looked…huggable.

Damn, what was that about?

He attributed it to knowing that she kissed like heaven, and smelled like it, too.

Then Matt opened his office door and smiled absently at her. "Yes?"

She bit her lower lip, clearly expecting a different reaction. "I wanted…to talk about last night."

"The party?" Matt seemed surprised.

The nitwit had no idea what he'd missed. Bryan supposed there should be some guilt associated with that, but there wasn't.

"I thought it went really well," Matt said, then stole a quick glance at his watch. "Oh, look at that. I'm sorry, I've gotta go. I have a report to finish."

With an apologetic smile, he turned away to shut the door.

"But—" Katie's smile seemed forced, even to Bryan who was still a good way down the hall from them. "It's just that…the mistletoe…"

"Mistletoe?" Matt shrugged. "I noticed plenty of the stuff scattered all around. The decorations were superbly done. Nicely and strategically placed."

"Yes," Katie agreed. *"Strategic."*

"It's got to come down though, or we'll have people taking advantage of it during office hours." His brow wrinkled. "Hmm...maybe I'd better write a memo."

"A memo," Katie repeated. "Remove the mistletoe to avoid mass orgies during work hours."

Matt nodded distractedly, and after a quick goodbye, closed the door in her face.

Clueless jerk, Bryan decided, even as he was oddly grateful for clueless jerks.

Katie just stood there. "Well wasn't I ever so memorable," she muttered.

More than memorable, babe. "Morning," Bryan said.

Katie nearly leaped right out of her skin and whipped around to stare at him. "What?"

"I said, 'Morning.'"

Her face was pale now. "Say it again."

Bryan wondered if his voice was confusing her. After all, he *had* spoken last night. But people heard what they wanted to hear, and she'd definitely wanted to hear Matt's voice.

She blinked.

"Morning," he said again, obliging her.

She shook her head. "I should have had some coffee."

And he should tell her the truth. *Should* being the key word here. "You were asking about the mistletoe," he said. "Is there something I can help you with?" *Like maybe kiss you again?*

She didn't answer, just narrowed her eyes.

"Is anything wrong?"

"Your voice…it sounds…"

"Familiar?" He grinned, he couldn't help it. "Well, it should. We work together."

"Right."

Poor baby looked so confused. His conscience, never the most righteous of creatures, reared its head for a moment.

A very short moment.

Because he knew if he came clean right then, she would either deny that the kiss had knocked her socks off, or she'd run like hell.

Neither appealed.

Not when his goal for the day had suddenly become to get another. "About that mistletoe," he said casually. "I bet it's still in the hangar. We could just walk on over there and—"

"No," she said quickly, backing away. "I'm… busy. Very busy."

He obviously made her nervous. He tested this theory by taking a step toward her.

Sure enough, she retreated…right into a file cab-

inet, which she hit with a loud thunk. The two flow-
erpots above teetered wildly, then fell. She caught
one, then the other, and quickly set them down on
the ground, whirling back to him with her hands
behind her back as if she didn't trust herself.

She had a streak of dirt across one cheek. She
looked unsettled. And adorable. He had no idea
why that appealed, he'd certainly never been attracted to adorable before. Long-legged, full bot-
tom-lipped sexpots, yes. Adorable, no.

"I'm fine," she said quickly when he came toward her. "I'm just fi—" The word ended in a gasp
when he took her arms in his hands to steady her.

They were now in exactly the same position
they'd been in last night, nose to nose, thigh to
thigh.

"You—you have blue eyes," she said inanely.
"When did that happen?"

"At birth, actually." He grinned. "Let me guess,
you hate blue eyes."

"No, I—" Her gaze dropped to his mouth, and
in a totally innocent gesture, she licked her dry lips.

Bryan nearly groaned, but managed to hold it
together because he had a huge advantage—*she*
might not know how good they'd be together, but
he did. Dammit, what a dilemma, because despite
himself, he never, ever took advantage of women.

Well, almost never.

"About that mistletoe…" he murmured.

"No! No, it was a bad idea! A stupid idea. A really idiotic—"

"I get the picture." He tipped his head to one side because her hands had come up between them to grip his shirt, whether to push him away or to keep him close, he had no idea. "You don't strike me as much of a risk taker."

"Absolutely not," she said quickly. Too quickly.

He smiled, because last night, for whatever reason, she'd done exactly that, she'd dropped her reserve and had made the first move on a man. On *him.*

"In fact, *risk* is a bad word in my book," she continued. "A really bad word, as bad as—as—"

"As…?"

"As…oh never mind!"

Above them, the intercom buzzed, then Mrs. Giddeon paged Katie to the front desk.

With a cry of what could only be relief, Katie broke free, brushing against him as she ran off down the hall.

Good, Bryan decided. He shouldn't have teased her. He had absolutely no idea what had come over him. He could really care less that she wanted Matt, that she wasn't his type. It wasn't his problem.

Five minutes later he walked into his office and faced his two other pilots, both of whom looked at him and laughed. He looked down.

And saw two perfect handprints—made from dirt—on his white shirt. "Very funny," he said, but he wasn't annoyed, just strangely unsettled.

Katie might be a novice where men were concerned, but she'd accomplished something no woman other than his sisters and mother ever had.

She'd left her mark on him.

3

"LORDIE, would you look at that?" Julie murmured beneath her breath to Katie.

At the voice of her friend and co-worker, Katie looked up from her notes for the upcoming staff meeting, but she saw nothing out of the ordinary.

Cassandra and Eloise filed into the conference room, followed by Dale, Jack, Evan and Mrs. Giddeon. Everyone looked perfectly normal, even Holly, as she sauntered in.

Then she caught the newest arrival.

Bryan.

That her belly gave a little quiver really got to her. "Him?" she asked Julie, who was practically drooling.

"*Him,*" Julie answered breathlessly. "Wow."

Granted he was tall, dark and…okay, gorgeous. So what? And yet for some reason that only upped her annoyance factor, she couldn't take her eyes off him. Even worse, she was hit with a strange sense of…*awareness?*

She didn't understand it, but she didn't appear to suffer the enigmatic problem alone. Apparently every female in the room was afflicted. Even Holly, who managed to maneuver herself close to him.

Watch out, Katie wanted to warn him. Holly was looking as predatory as she had...oh, about one minute before she'd stolen Katie's fiancé three years ago.

Beneath her own Christmas tree no less.

Old times, she reminded herself. Forget it.

And anyway, *where was Matt?*

She'd been hoping for a few minutes alone with him to discuss their kiss. It'd been three days!

But still, she couldn't tear her gaze away from Bryan. She had to admit the man had a presence. The very air around him seemed to change, shimmer with an aura of excitement. Thrill.

Danger.

That presence wasn't put on, like it was with so many daredevils. Nope, all that edgy restlessness came utterly naturally to him.

Which was exactly why Katie didn't—couldn't—like him.

"There's something not quite tame about that man," Julie announced in a conspirator's whisper. She shivered with delight.

To Katie there was nothing even remotely exciting about it. Her father had flown stunts. He'd done things no one else would even consider and had *still* craved more, even putting aside the needs of his own family in order to get it. He'd been grown-up enough to have a family, but not mature enough to want to be with that family. Her father was always pushing the envelope, and always going full speed ahead. Always wanting, craving, yearning, burning for something just out of his reach.

He'd found it in testing experimental aircraft.

Oh, and it had also killed him.

Katie tried to swallow the nearly twenty-year-old resentment and only managed to swallow her last piece of gum, which left a heavy feeling in the pit of her stomach.

She could never fall for a man like that, one who wasn't mature enough to put fun on the back burner in the favor of a quiet, lasting, enduring relationship.

Julie looked at her. ''Are you telling me you don't think he's spectacular?''

Well, she was human. *Female* human. She could admit Bryan's broad shoulders, so perfectly covered in his white pilot's shirt, were nice, very nice indeed. So were his long, long, powerfully built legs, which were in dark-blue trousers fitted in a way that might have made her sigh in feminine appreciation if she was weak enough to sigh over such things. He had his aviator sunglasses tucked in his front pocket, his sleeves shoved up instead of rolled, and scuffed work boots on his feet. His hair was tousled as if he'd been running his fingers through it.

Gorgeously rumpled, she supposed was the correct term.

But it was his face that held her; the rugged, tanned, lived-in face. The one that had laugh lines around his generous mouth and smile creases around his sharp eyes, eyes that told her what she needed to know—he actively recruited fun and trouble, and—

Darn it.

He caught her staring at him.

No surprise, no discomfort, not for this man, who was probably used to being stared at. He merely absorbed her gaze, gave her a quick wink and a slow grin.

And in spite of her embarrassment and irritation, something strange happened. Something…almost familiar.

What was it about him?

Why did she feel as if…they *knew* each other? As if she'd kissed *him* instead of Matt? She nearly laughed out loud at that, because really, she knew who she'd kissed.

Matt stepped into the room then, a very welcome sight indeed. His hair was perfectly groomed, his shirt perfectly ironed, his trousers perfectly styled.

Everything about him was perfect.

Only, oddly enough, the little flicker of awareness, the one Bryan had caused, died. *Died.*

And Katie went cold.

She *had* kissed Matt. Right? Well, of course she had, what a ridiculous notion, one she put right out of her thoughts. Instead, she concentrated on smiling a welcome smile. Only Matt's nose was in his notes and without even glancing in her direction, he sat directly across from her. He was distracted, she decided, and very busy. She understood that. Still, her smile faded with the slight, unintentional as it was.

Yes, Matt was the perfect man for her, but she did expect to get noticed at least. Determined to get a reaction, she pasted on a new smile. "Hello, Matt."

"Hmm?" Matt lifted his head, blinked her into focus. "Oh. Hello." He even returned her smile, blossoming her hopes, but then he went back to his notes.

Sedate and mature were fine qualities, but this was getting ridiculous. "I was wondering about the party." This time he didn't so much as lift his head

from his work, and Katie went from vexed to insulted. "And the decorations," she added. "Specifically the mistletoe."

Matt sent her an absent smile at that. His face
was open, easy to read and utterly serene. Nothing
bothered him, or very little. He was a peaceful,
quiet, reserved man. *The perfect man,* she reminded
herself.

So why did she feel like smacking him? Oh, yes,
because he wasn't acknowledging their hot kiss!

"The mistletoe was a great idea," he allowed.
"I already mentioned that."

"Yes, but—"

"For God's sake man, she's trying to ask you
about the *use* of it." Bryan merely smiled sweetly
at Katie when she stared at him. "Aren't you?"

"I...well..." *How did he know?* And why was
she feeling *that* feeling again, the one that made her
insides tremble, the one she had thought *Matt*
would give her?

Holly laughed, the sound easy and infectious.
"Wasn't it a grand party? I know for a fact that
every single one of those strategically hung plants
got good use." She smiled slyly at Matt, who
blushed.

Blushed!

Katie stared at him in dismay. For days she'd

been attempting to get a reaction from him and had gotten nothing. Then Holly says one little thing and he blushes! Frustrated, she glared down at her stack of notes, mail and various pencils and stuff she'd brought with her to the meeting.

Her heavy silver mail opener gleamed temptingly in the harsh office lights.

No, killing Holly right here would not be good office protocol, she decided, not even when the darn woman brushed part of Katie's paperwork off the table.

"Oops," Holly said lightly as everything scattered and entangled on the floor. She glanced over at Matt as she spoke to Katie. "Sorry."

Katie glared at her—she'd done that on purpose!—but Holly didn't notice, she was still staring at Matt. So Katie bent for the mess, and from her vantage point beneath the table, she had a front row seat of Holly slipping off her right heel and lifting her toes up to…Bryan's lap! Her bright-red polished toes cradled the spot directly between his thighs…and squeezed.

He made a sound, though it was muffled to Katie because she was beneath the table. She watched as Bryan's hand grabbed Holly's ankle, his fingers gripping so hard his knuckles turned white.

They were playing hanky-panky, right here in the

conference room and she had to witness it! Holly slid off her other heel, then lifted that leg up to Bryan's lap as well.

Katie jerked back...and smacked her head on the underside of the table hard enough to rattle everyone's water above. Whether it was the impact, or the resulting stars dancing in her head, or maybe the strangled sound Bryan made at the movement of Holly's toes, Katie bit her tongue. "Ouch," she muttered, just as Holly played twinkle toes with Bryan's lap again.

Abruptly, he shoved back his chair and rose. He gathered his paperwork, and without another word, walked around the table.

Katie figured he'd sit right next to Holly, maybe for some more footsie action, but no such luck. He came around, passed Holly and sat...right next to Katie!

"Wow, he smells amazing," Julie whispered in her ear.

Holly leaned across the table to Katie. "Switch spots with me, quick."

Katie glanced at Bryan. He was looking a little ragged around the edges, and more than a little tense. A very unusual look for Mr. Casual.

"If you switch with her," he said mildly, "I'll tell Matt why you keep bringing up the mistletoe."

Okay, switching was probably a bad idea.

But how did Bryan know that?

She blinked at him, considering, thoughts racing, and Bryan just sent her a slow, sure smile, a smile that tugged at every erogenous zone she had.

What was the matter with her?

Thankfully, Mr. Riggs, president and director of Wells Aviation, walked into the room then and Katie had other, more critical things to stress over.

Such as why she spent the next hour sniffing as unobtrusively as she could, obsessing over the fact that Julie had been correct.

Bryan did indeed smell pretty darn amazing.

BRYAN COULDN'T GET OUT of that meeting fast enough, couldn't get outside, in the fresh chilly air, soon enough to suit him.

With relief, he headed for his scheduled flight, loving every moment of the next few hours as he charmed his passengers, then flew high in the air, in sweet control.

All too soon he was back in the lobby.

So was Holly.

''What was that about back there?'' he demanded in a quiet but dangerous voice most people had the good sense to answer.

She played her tongue over the very corner of

her mouth in a way Bryan was sure rendered most males completely stupid. Fortunately he was only slightly less stupid than the average man. "Holly."

She smiled. "You mean when I put my foot on your—"

"You know that's what I mean."

"I could tell you liked it."

So she had talented toes. "I want to know why you're using me, and who you're trying to make jealous."

"Well that's flattering."

"Don't play games with me."

"But games are so much fun."

"I don't get it," he said, genuinely baffled. "Why don't you just go straight after whoever he is? I'm sure he'd fall right at your feet as all men do."

"*You* haven't."

"But you don't want me," he pointed out, exasperated.

"Are you sure?"

This was why he kept women at arm's length. But being the baby of a family with so many females, he'd been taught well. The last thing he needed was to let Holly—or any woman—get to him. Still annoyed, he looked through the glass windows and across the tarmac.

A figure walked behind the safety line toward hangar two.

Katie.

The most unusual thing happened. His heart stopped, then started again with a heavy beat. He found himself staring after her, which made no sense, no sense at all.

But there was something about her...

On impulse, he walked away from Holly without a backward glance and followed the flash of blue. He finally caught up with her in the long hallway between the mechanic's hangar and the supply warehouse.

"Hey there," he said.

She didn't slow down, and he had to practically run to keep up with her. "Nice office meeting," he said.

Nice office meeting.

Oh, wasn't he just the conversation master? Grimacing, he shook his head and tried again. "You look pretty today." Which was true, though he wished she would trade in those conservative outfits for something better suited to her petite yet curvaceous frame.

"Holly looks prettier," she noted, still walking at nearly the speed of light. "If you tell her so, she'll probably be so flattered you'll be able to grope her back this time.''

"What?" He stopped to gape at her, but all that accomplished was to allow her to outdistance him. Her hips and sweet rear end were really moving now. Running to catch back up, he grabbed her arm to slow her down and turned her to face him.

"I said, if you tell her so," she repeated dutifully. "You might—"

"I heard that part!" He must have missed something here. Katie's face, usually calm, flashed annoyance, anger, even embarrassment.

The lightbulb finally clicked on in his dim-witted brain. "Holly told you about what she did—"

"No, I *saw* what she did, when she dropped my papers and I went under the table. I saw her foot— And then you— Oh, you know!"

Yeah, he knew. "Don't you see what's happening?" He was disturbed that she really didn't appear to. And even more disgusted that it mattered so much to him. Since when did he care what people thought?

But he cared what *she* thought, he realized, and figured he'd dwell on that shocking fact later. "You saw exactly what Holly wanted you to."

"What do you mean?"

He hated this. It was like being back in high

school, and he'd really hated high school. He'd thought to wait to tell Katie the truth about the Santa thing, both because it amused him to keep the secret and because he took few things seriously other than flying.

But oddly enough, he was taking this very seriously. "I know you're trying to get Matt to discuss your Christmas party kiss, but there's a good reason he won't."

"I know." She grimaced. "It's because I'm Christmas cursed. I never should have made that stupid Christmas wish."

"You're…Christmas cursed?"

"Let's just say Santa seems to lose my address."

"And the Christmas wish thing?"

"It's no big deal."

"Oh, I think it probably is."

"Okay, fine, I made a stupid wish to…" She blushed. "Can I ask you something?"

"Of course."

"Well, you're a man…"

"Yes." He had to smile. "That was too easy, try another question."

She rolled her eyes. "Forget it, just forget it. It's not important."

Yes, it was, he could see that much. But so was this. "About that kiss, Katie—"

"I'd like to forget that, too."

"Sorry, no can do." He'd never forget it. "Matt can't discuss this with you. He can't, Katie, because *I'm* the one who shared that kiss with you."

Her mouth worked.

Opened.

Closed.

Opened again. "I kissed Matt," she finally managed to say. "In the Santa costume."

"No. You kissed me. In the Santa costume. And I think you already know it."

"No."

"Yes. Otherwise, how would I know about it?" He tried to smile, but truthfully the memory of her in that dress, pressed against him, her mouth on his, pretty much made it difficult. "I know if you think about it, you'll see the truth. You've nearly recognized me every single day since."

"In your dreams."

"Really? Then why are you always staring at me?"

"I am *not* always staring at you!"

When he only waited patiently, she blew out a frustrated breath. "Much," she muttered.

"I'm flattered," he said.

"Don't be! I did not kiss you!"

"I could prove it to you, if you'd like."

4

He could prove it to her.

Oh, Lord.

Katie's palms were clammy, her heart raced.

The flu, she decided. It was just the flu coming on.

Which didn't explain why the thought of him "proving it" to her had her nipples hard and achy.

Bryan kept his distance, but she felt the heat of him, the power in his big frame all the same, and she knew if she slid her arms around his neck and pressed close he'd make a rough, appreciative growl—

No. This was most definitely a road she did not want to travel.

Normally she was an easygoing person. Quiet and reserved, maybe even a little mousy, but she was working on that. And yet she wasn't easygoing now. "How could you prove something that never happened?" she asked with remarkable—and totally false—calm.

"By kissing you again."

She stared at him, and it wasn't a loss of words that made speaking difficult, but that she had so much to say and no rationale left in which to say it. "No, you can't kiss me."

"Again. You mean I can't kiss you *again*."

"There was never a first time!"

He leaned closer so that she was surrounded by him. "I have six sisters," he confided in a voice that managed to convey both his affection and love for his family. "That's six nosy, bossy, demanding and completely wonderful *females*."

She did not want to know this about him. She wanted to picture him as wild, uncaring and...well, a jerk.

He felt safer that way.

But nothing about this man was safe. Nothing.

"So trust me on this one," he continued. "I learned early to never disagree with a woman, but I'm very sorry to say you're wrong."

Did he have to stand so close? She could see his eyes weren't just a *little* blue, but all the way, ocean-deep, drown-in-me blue. Terrific. Not only did he love his family, but he had amazing eyes.

Not fair.

He also had a scar that ran along the line of his dark brow, probably from doing something crazy.

Realizing she was staring at him, and that he was enjoying that very thing, she turned on her heels and moved toward the storage warehouse. She didn't need anything, but she felt so flustered, so uncustomarily unnerved, she opened it, flipped on the light and stepped inside.

Okay, think.

She'd kissed Santa Claus, she knew this much for certain. The rest was pure speculation. She knew what she wanted. She wanted Santa to have been Matt. Wanted *Matt* to have hoarsely whispered her name with longing. Wanted *Matt* to have been the one to put his hands on her and gently squeeze as if he could never get enough of her.

Nice, dependable, kind Matt. Grown-up Matt. Perfect Matt.

She had no doubt it had been him, none whatsoever.

None.

Mostly none.

This wasn't good. In fact, this was bad, very bad.

"You're thinking about it, aren't you?" Bryan whispered.

"No."

"Liar."

"If you have six sisters, you also know it's not exactly flattering to call a woman a liar."

He grinned.

"I bet you're the baby of the family," she said without thinking, and his grin widened.

"Oh, I am. Spoiled rotten, too. And you know what else? You're interested in me. I like that." He settled even closer and smiled at her. "What else can I tell you?"

"Why you'd want to play footsy with Holly."

His smile faded. *Honestly* faded. "Holly is the last person on earth I would play footsy with," he said. "That woman is dangerous."

"Men like that."

"Men like excitement, not danger, not in a woman anyway."

"Uh-huh," she said in a tone that could be construed as nothing other than sarcasm.

"Tell me this much," he said, strangely intent. "Did you see me egging her on? Or did you see me move away from her as quickly as I could?"

She thought about that. "You moved away from her."

"Like a mouse out of a snake's path."

That made her laugh. "You're hardly a mouse." But she could concede that maybe what she'd seen in the meeting *had* been one-sided. There were, however, other issues here. Personal issues. Bryan may be charming when he wanted, but he wasn't serious. At least not about women. And she *was* serious. She wanted a *serious* man.

"Ask me something else," he encouraged. "Go on, try me."

"Okay…why did you take that terribly dangerous stunt job yesterday morning?"

"It wasn't that dangerous."

"I watched you pull out of that spin with only seconds to spare." She hadn't meant to say it, hadn't meant to sound so worried.

"You watched."

Oh, yeah, she'd watched. Watched and bitten her nails down to the quick with anxiety she hadn't wanted to feel. "You fly with wild, reckless abandon."

"Thank you."

"That wasn't a compliment!"

"I'm careful, and highly skilled."

He was talented, she'd give him that. "I just don't know why you have to do it like that, as if each second was going to be your last."

"Katie, I *live* like that."

She backed up until she came up against a shelving unit, which she gripped at her sides with fisted hands. "*Exactly.* You live like that. Which is the reason…which is why—" Horrified, she broke off.

"Why what? Why you can't admit it was me you kissed?"

How to explain that she had a precise definition of what she wanted in a man and he was the exact opposite? She wanted the three *S*'s. Security, safety, stability. She didn't want to be afraid for his life on a daily basis. She didn't want someone who made her feel as if she were on a perpetual roller coaster.

She hated roller coasters!

As if he could read her mind, his good humor vanished, replaced by an intensity she didn't know how to handle, and he once again closed the distance between them. Now she could feel the warmth of his breath on her temple as he quietly studied her. "Was it that bad? The kiss?"

She studied her shoes. The ceiling. The wall. Anything other than his serious and oh-so-gorgeous face.

But he didn't give up.

"Did I kiss like a Saint Bernard?" he asked. "Did I have breath like a whale? What?"

She couldn't help it, she laughed. "I'm not admitting anything, mind you, but no, not bad breath. Not too much slobber. It was…"

"Yes?"

"A twenty on a scale of one to ten," she admitted.

He smiled, not a cocky one, but it still made her roll her eyes and look away. Until he caught her chin in his fingers and turned her back to him.

"Why don't you like me?" he asked softly, and when she opened her mouth to deny this, he gently slid those fingers against her lips.

At his touch, a bewildering tightness invaded her insides. Her eyes widened on his. She saw his jaw tighten, felt his fingers tense, and wondered if he felt the same confusion.

"Truth," he whispered. "For months and months now you've done your damnedest to avoid me. Changing directions in the hallway, sitting far away in staff meetings, dealing with my pilots when you need something, instead of dealing with me. Why, Katie? At least tell me why."

One last stroke with his fingers and then he lifted them away from her lips, but he didn't move, so that when she tipped her head up to look at him, her mouth was only inches from his. It shocked her to realize her body was straining closer to him, and once again she flattened herself against the shelving unit. "It's not that I don't like you. But we have nothing in common."

"How do you figure?"

"Well, other than us being day and night? Oil and vinegar—"

"*Concrete* reasons. No cheating with silly metaphors."

"Okay, well…I'm plain. And you're—" *Outrageously sexy.* "*Not* plain," she finished lamely.

"Neither are you."

"Then you're too tall."

He laughed. "Chicken excuse, but I'll let you have it. What else?"

"I like everything planned out."

"And I don't?"

"You'd jump off a cliff on a whim."

"If I had a good rope, maybe."

"See? Polar opposites. That's us."

"That's not completely true." His voice was low, husky, his direct gaze like a caress. "We both love airplanes."

"How—" How could he have known about her secret passion and love of planes? That she hoarded and devoured every book she could find, every picture, every magazine. That sometimes, late at night, she wandered through the hangars and just looked at the planes that so fascinated and terrified her at the same time?

"I've seen you." He lifted a finger and tucked a wayward strand of hair behind her ear. The touch electrified her. "I've seen the look of longing and passion on your face as you've touched a sleek

Lear, seen your yearning. Why don't you fly, Katie? What keeps you grounded?''

''My father,'' she confided before she could stop herself, and this time it was *her* who covered *his* mouth. ''Don't. Don't ask, I don't want to talk about it.''

His hand came up and circled her wrist. When he spoke, his lips tickled her palm. ''We should.''

''No. Look, it's nothing personal.''

''I think it is.''

''I just...'' Lord, it was hard to think. She had her hand on his mouth, his very *sexy* mouth, and she couldn't tear her gaze from it, even when it curved with satisfaction. ''I'm not much of a risk taker.''

His eyes sparkled at that. ''You're here alone in the warehouse with me, aren't you? Seems pretty risky to me. Tell me, what drew you to Santa that night? What made you want to kiss him?''

''I'm not going to tell you that!''

''Please?''

''This is silly. It doesn't matter to you.''

''Tell me.''

''It was Matt.''

''Matt.''

''Yes. He's dependable. Reliable. He's—''

''Mr. Perfect.'' He shook his head even as a

smile tugged at the corners of his mouth. "I've heard the women talk about him."

"Then you already knew what attracted me."

"Dependability? Reliability?" He made a face. "Sounds like a car. A new one, when we all know it's the *used* models, the coveted and experienced and loved ones, that have all the nerve and personality."

"Bryan—"

His eyes flashed now, still with good humor, but with something more as well. "*I* was Santa, Katie. And I'm going to prove it to you."

"No!" Not stopping to think about her sudden, irrational fear, Katie ducked from between the shelving unit and his body, not stopping to look at him until she had the door handle firmly in her hand and opened.

Bryan lifted his hands. "I wasn't going to prove it *that* way."

"Oh." She felt dense. "I just thought—"

"I know what you thought. That I was going to kiss you again. But if I wasn't Santa that night, if I wasn't the one to give you that kiss—which must have been a helluva doozy, by the way, to have made such an impression—you have nothing to worry about, right?"

"Um…yeah. Right."

He laughed softly then, a terrifyingly sexy sound that made the butterflies go to town on Katie's stomach again.

"How about I prove to you that it *was* me, but in another way?" he suggested.

Warily she eyed him. "How?"

"And when I do—" he completely ignored her question "—you're going to admit you were wrong. Out loud this time. To *me*."

She still had one foot out the door. She was safe. Yeah, safe as a name caller in a glass house. "I have no problem admitting my mistakes," she said so stiffly he laughed again. "But I'm not wrong here."

"Uh-huh. We'll see. Dependability. Reliability? Those are the things you need?"

"Yes," she whispered.

He looked slightly disgusted, but resigned. "Damn. I was afraid you were going to say that."

A FEW DAYS LATER, Bryan was in the middle of a final check, trying to get out of Wells for the day, when he heard a strange noise coming from the opened cockpit of his plane.

He set down his clipboard and walked around the Cessna, his mind a million miles away.

He was thinking fondly of mistletoe and sexy red

Christmas dresses. He was thinking of warm, vulnerable, whiskey-colored eyes, and sweet-scented, shoulder-length hair brushing over his arms as he leaned into the kiss that had rocked his world.

Was *still* rocking his world.

It had been a week.

Seven days.

One-hundred-sixty-eight hours.

He didn't know how many minutes, but for an admitted adrenaline junkie, he was dying for another rush.

Another kiss.

He'd tried his damnedest to appear to be the model citizen whenever Katie was around. Dependable. Reliable.

He did it all.

He tried so hard his head hurt. What was he doing? Why did he even care? Was he that egotistical that he couldn't let it go?

So Katie wanted neat and simple Matt, who was sedate enough to put a gorilla to sleep without effort.

In contrast, she thought Bryan wild. Uncontrollable.

That sound came from the cockpit again, and he climbed up the landing stairs of the sleek plane to peek inside.

Nothing.

He went in, took a step toward the cockpit, then froze when the door slammed behind him.

"What the—" He turned back just as a soft weight plowed into him. "Oof." The backs of his knees hit a low seat, tripping him, and he crashed into the wall of the plane.

On the floor, with his legs still draped over the back of the seat and that soft weight draped over the top of him, Bryan shook his head and evaluated.

Hot flesh and overly scented skin? "Holly! What the hell—"

That was the last word he managed before she straddled him, leaned in and whispered, "Take it like a man, would you? I need to use you for a second."

"What—"

"Hush! He's coming. I want him to see!" And she took his mouth with hers.

Behind them the airplane door opened abruptly and Katie's voice called into the dark depths. "Bryan?"

Both he and Holly swore.

"Matt's there, too!" Holly hissed. "Damn that man, he's so slow!"

"Bryan?" called Katie. "I need an invoice…."

Oh, perfect.

Bryan tried to jerk free, but Holly was quicker, and prepared. She pressed down on him, both with her knee in his windpipe and her mouth on his.

Worrying about Katie seeing the kiss became secondary to actually breathing. And still he heard Katie come closer.

Inanely, Bryan wondered if she would believe he'd passed out and Holly was performing mouth-to-mouth resuscitation. Certainly she'd never believe the truth, that he'd been attacked!

Hell, *he* hardly believed it.

"Bryan—" Katie's voice stopped short on an audible gasp as she caught sight of him—big, bad Bryan Morgan, being held to the floor by Holly's lips.

Dammit! Struggling to sit up, he shoved Holly off his thighs.

Katie was already halfway across the hangar floor.

Surging to his feet, he leaped for the door. "Katie!" he bellowed.

She turned, just as Bryan took a quick step, too quick, and promptly fell out of the plane, flat on his face.

When the stars and pain faded, he rolled onto his back on the cold concrete floor of the hangar and blinked Holly into view.

"Save your breath," she said with a sigh. "She's gone. For such a well-curved little thing, she sure can move. And apparently Matt wasn't with her."

Bryan spared her one quick glance as he surged to his unsteady feet. "You. *Stay.* When I get back you have some explaining to do."

"Oh, Ricky," she whined in a perfect mimic of Lucy Ricardo.

Instead of strangling her, Bryan shook his head and went after Katie, but Holly happened to be right on one score—Katie *could* really move.

By the time he figured out which way to go, she'd crossed the entire length of the tarmac, her low, economical heels clicking loudly, her long skirt flowing wildly in the breeze.

"Katie!"

Naturally she kept walking, even faster now, and he jogged up to her, passing her, running backwards in order to stay right in front of her, but she wouldn't even look at him. "Katie, I—"

"I'm busy," she huffed.

"You're also upset."

"Why? I don't care who you kiss."

Ouch, though it was a good point. She didn't care, he didn't care...so what was the big deal?

He wished he knew.

His face hurt from taking a dive on the hangar

floor. His head hurt, too, and though he was in excellent shape, he could hardly keep up with her. "Can you stop for a moment? Or at least slow down?"

"Nope."

He glanced behind him to make sure he wasn't going to fall, *again,* and kept running backward. "About what just happened—"

"Forget it."

He'd like to. "I can't. You know, it wasn't really what you thought."

"Really?" Finally, she stopped, put a hand on her hip and lifted an eyebrow. "What did I think?"

"Um…" He was feeling a little slow on the uptake.

"That you're slime? That you're sick? That you're— You're bleeding!"

Why that softened her, he hadn't a clue.

"Your lip," she said and lifted a hand before she stopped herself. "You should tell your little girlfriend not to bite so hard."

"She's not—" Hell! How did this stuff happen to him?

They were on the far side of the tarmac now, the wind blowing fiercely, whipping Katie's hair into both of their faces. Her skirt rioted, too, tangling up in his legs as well as hers. They were close to the lobby door, close to the first hangar, but neither of them moved. "I suppose you won't believe the truth," he said.

Her gaze narrowed and now she did touch his mouth and stared at her finger. Then she stabbed it into his chest, hard. "That's not blood, it's bright red lipstick! Gee, I wonder how *that* happened? Oh, wait, I know." She let out a tight smile. "You're a closet cross-dresser."

"She jumped me," he said inanely, going with the truth instead of the resuscitation excuse, thinking he should get points for honesty. "Really. I heard this noise and went to investigate."

"In your parked plane."

"Yes."

"I imagine you thought it was a mouse or something."

"Or something, yes," he agreed, ignoring her huff of disbelief. "Then suddenly there she was, kissing me."

"She plowed you to the ground, naturally," Katie said agreeably. "Straddled you. Forced your arms around her, then attacked your mouth."

Pleased by her compassion and understanding, he smiled. "Yes! Exactly!"

Katie's eyes went cold. "Someone ought to put out a bulletin. You men need a new story."

"What are you talking about?"

"That's exactly the same story my fiancé gave me, when I found him in the same position with Holly. Only it was under my Christmas tree, three years ago."

5

FOR THE FIRST TIME in Katie's life, her nice, logical world of accounting failed her. She had her computer up and running, a spreadsheet opened in front of her and yet all she saw were numbers leaping and jumping around, making her dizzy.

She found herself mixing her debits with her credits. Confusing her assets with liabilities. Twisting her expenses.

All because of a man. And not the man she'd so carefully picked out for herself either, but one who had the ability to turn her life upside down in a very unsettling way.

How was she supposed to face the fact that the kiss that haunted her dreams with its heat and intensity, the one that had awakened needs and yearnings she hadn't even been aware of, might have come from a man she could never let herself care about?

Never.

Bryan was everything she didn't want. Unpredictable. Wild. Uncontrollable.

Not to mention a woman magnet.

Anyway, it didn't matter, she'd kissed Matt.

She really had.

Oh, Lord. Her head hit the desk with a loud
thunk.

Not Bryan, please don't let it be true.

She was happy with her life just the way it was.
Mostly. Okay, she was working on the happy part.
But what she wanted for the rest of it was quite
simple—the exact opposite of what Bryan made her
feel. Her three little *S*'s.

Security, safety, stability.

All three of those in one, Matt poked his head in
her office door and smiled.

She lifted her head and smiled back, stupidly,
yearning for his next words.

*I'm sorry I've been teasing you, of course I re-
member our kiss.*

Or better yet, *How about we try that bone-
melting kiss again because for the life of me I can't
stop thinking about it.*

Actually, if he could just haul her out of her
chair, press his body to hers and plant one on her...
Yeah, now *that* would be the best thing to lay to
rest all these crazy doubts.

With that in mind, she waited earnestly.

"We need the general ledger," he said, shattering her hopes with quiet ease. "Do you by any chance have it ready?"

Maybe he was just shy. She could understand that, really she could. But right now she was desperately afraid she knew why he wasn't responding to her, darn one Bryan Morgan!

She had to know, without a shadow of a doubt, who she'd kissed.

"It's almost ready," she lied, purposely not looking down at her desk, where the thing lay out right in the open, finished. "Why don't you come in for a second while I get it?"

"Okay."

"Oh, and maybe you could shut the door?"

He did, and then leaned against her file cabinet, tall and lean. Handsome. Reliable. Dependable.

A mental image of a car salesman flashed in her mind and she shoved it out.

Matt was Mr. Perfect, and she was going to prove it to herself if it killed her.

As she walked toward him, some of her intent and purpose must have gleamed in her gaze because he straightened, his brow crinkled in question.

She kept walking, afraid she'd lose her nerve.

Matt abandoned his perch and backed up, until her extra chair hit the back of his knees, forcing him to sit. He gripped the arms and sent her a wary look. "Um...how about I come back later when—"

When she was in her right mind?

Not likely to happen.

"No need," she said, putting her hands over his as she bent, lowering her face, puckering her lips, not quite daring to close her eyes because she was nervous and deathly afraid she'd miss her target.

"Katie!" Matt scooted back as far as he could in the chair, but she had him surrounded. The chair made an alarming squeak, then started to tip with his efforts as she tried to soothe him.

"Just one more time, Matt."

"One more time? *What are you taking about?*"

Her palms grew damp with nerves, making them slip on the armrests. She fell across his lap full weight.

"Oomph," he said, and though she tried to smile a come-hither smile, he didn't put his hands on her as she imagined, instead arched even farther away from her as she fumbled. "Katie—"

That was the last word he managed before their combined weight proved too much for the chair. They toppled backward to the floor.

THE HOSPITAL waiting room had been painted a soft green, and decorated with warm paintings and drawings.

Probably to calm people.

It wasn't working, a half hysterical Katie was certain of that much. Nope, in fact that green was making her feel seasick.

Of course it could have been that she'd nearly killed the vice president of Wells Aviation.

"A concussion," Bryan said from his chair, watching her pace. "How do you suppose *that* happened?"

She cringed and kept pacing.

"He's a careful man," Bryan said thoughtfully. "I can't imagine him just…falling out of his chair."

"Um, yeah. About that…" Katie managed a little smile. "He didn't exactly fall on his own."

"I see." Though his mouth remained still, his eyes twinkled with what she was pretty certain was humor. "You mean something tipped him over?"

"Sort of." Katie closed her eyes in mortification. "You remember that Christmas party thing?"

Now one corner of his mouth quirked. "I think I do, yes."

"And that stupid kiss."

Bryan paused so long Katie opened her eyes.

"That stupid kiss," he repeated.

"It should have been so simple!" She forced a laugh. "It's really the funniest thing."

"Try me."

"Well, I got to thinking about what you said, you know, about it not being Matt."

Bryan just looked at her.

"Right. Anyway, I got to wondering—"

"If I was telling the truth? I thought we already established that much. If I wasn't, how would I even know about the kiss?"

"Well, I didn't say I was rational." She managed another smile. "I needed to know for certain if it was really Matt, even though of course it was. You were just somehow teasing me. All I had to do was prove it, so I just..."

"You just...what?"

"Tried to kiss Matt again." She rubbed her eyes. "And that was that."

"Not quite it wasn't. You left out the part where you nearly killed him."

"Oh, yeah." She sank to an empty chair and dropped both her bravado and head into her hands.

"The headlines should be interesting," Bryan told her sympathetically. "'Accountant Launches Herself at Single Executive, Hoping for a Kiss and

Knocks Him Out Cold.' You know, in some states you could probably get arrested.''

That thought hadn't even occurred to her, but it did now and Katie went weak. If it had been the other way around, and Matt had been the woman, and *she* the *he*… ''Oh, God, I sexually harassed him!''

Bryan grinned. ''Shame on you. Can you do it to me, too?''

''I'm going to be sick,'' she said faintly.

''Well, this is the place to do it.'' But he ran his hand over her bowed head in a soothing gesture.

The craziest thought went through her mind at his oddly welcome touch. She was resisting him because…well, he wasn't grown-up enough, didn't know anything but fun. And yet here he was, being the mature one in the face of her own stupidity. She might have warmed to him then. Might have, except for his next words.

''Look, it's not that bad,'' he said. ''At least now you know the truth.''

''No,'' she said miserably. ''I never actually kissed him before we fell.''

Bryan stared at her, then laughed. ''You poor baby.''

"ARE YOU WAITING for Matt Osborne?"

Katie straightened in her chair and looked at the nurse in surprise. "Me?"

"He's been released. You're driving him home?"

Katie looked around, but there was no one else the woman could possibly be speaking to. Bryan had vanished a half hour ago. "Um...okay." Guess she wasn't fired.

Yet.

She followed the nurse down the hallway past the emergency room cubicles. Not all the curtains were closed so she got an eyeful of moaning, groaning, screaming, yelling people.

Not a happy place.

Finally they stopped before a cubicle that *did* have a closed curtain. The nurse whipped it open, and when Katie hesitated, the woman gently pushed her inside and slid the curtain closed again.

Matt sat on the cot, holding his head in his hands. When he saw her, he straightened, his eyes widening a little.

Terrific. Now he was afraid of her. She forced a smile. "Matt? They said you're free to go now."

"Yes." He looked at the closed curtain behind her as if it were a bolted steel door and he was locked on the wrong side of it.

The awkwardness didn't fade when she found her feet and moved closer to him. With a barely perceptible movement, he shifted back, away from her.

She dropped to the cot next to him and sighed. Any second now he'd fire her. She'd take it like a man.

Probably.

"Katie?" He sounded wary but concerned, which made her sigh again.

Mr. Perfect was a gentleman, right to the end. Except that he was watching her as one would a poisonous spider. She supposed she couldn't really blame him; in his eyes she'd been acting pretty strange since the party.

"Why are you here?" he asked.

"I'm driving you home." She attempted a friendly, don't-worry-I'm-sane smile. "I'll have you there in five minutes tops."

He looked as if five minutes were a lifetime. Or maybe he was just worried she'd knock him down again and *really* injure him this time.

Well, that was her own fault, she supposed. And she still wasn't any closer to the truth. He was so handsome, and so darn right for her!

Why couldn't this be simple?

Slowly she lifted a hand toward him, hoping he'd take it. He didn't, instead stared down at her fingers as if he expected them to separate from her body and yell *Boo!* "We really need to go," she said.

"Just checking…" He gingerly took her fingers, studying them intently. Then he slowly craned his neck and stared at the ceiling, and then the walls around him. "For mistletoe." He shot her an apologetic smile. "I'm sorry, it's just that you seem so obsessed…."

She tightened her grip on his hand and gently tugged him up because she *was* obsessed. And she wasn't finished; she had to know. She had to put the wild, unpredictable and far too sexy Bryan out of her head. "I have to try this one last time," she whispered, more to herself than him. "I won't hurt you, I promise." Going up on her tiptoes, she lightly pressed her mouth to his.

He stiffened at the connection, and she thought, *Yes!* because she'd felt the same reaction from him, at the party. But that night his hands had tightened on her, he'd made a rough sound of helpless arousal, and had immediately taken over the kiss until she couldn't so much as remember her name.

Not this time.

No fireworks, no heat barreling through her veins, nothing except the short, dry, chaste kiss.

Matt immediately pulled back and frowned at her. "What was *that* for?"

"Yes, Katie. Do tell."

Katie jerked around. *Bryan!* What? Was her good karma on vacation?

Bryan lifted a mocking eyebrow, darn him, and sent her a knowing smile.

"What are you doing here?" she demanded.

"Me?"

"Yes, you!"

"Matt asked me to drive him home." Bryan's eyes sparkled, his mouth quivered suspiciously. "Unless of course, *you're* going to do it."

"No!" Matt said quickly, too quickly, then sent Katie an apologetic but terrified glance.

Katie could only sigh. Bryan's eyes were still on her, she could feel them, but she'd streak naked through the hospital before she'd look at him again.

"Hope I didn't interrupt anything," he said lightly, turning her, forcing her to face him.

Oh, yes, given that smug expression, he knew *exactly* what he'd interrupted, and she'd never live it down.

His cocky, wicked grin only reinforced the knowledge.

6

WELL, AT LEAST she had Tic and Toc, her cats. They'd never abandon her. They'd never look at her with soft reproach as Matt had, wondering why she was trying to ruin his life.

Darn him for giving her a complex anyway. All she'd wanted was one little kiss; it wouldn't have hurt him to cooperate.

Much.

"Meow."

Katie let out a long, shaky breath. "Well, I didn't *mean* to hurt him," she told the cat. "But really, now that I think about it, that concussion was his own fault. If he would've just stayed still, we wouldn't have fallen."

She sat on her porch, both cats heavy in her lap as she watched the sunset and sighed. "I'm still Christmas cursed, apparently. Big surprise there."

"I've heard you say that twice now."

She nearly dumped Tic and Toc to the floor at the unexpected sound of his voice.

Bryan stood below the bottom step.

In the growing dark, she couldn't see his expression clearly, and told herself it wasn't necessary. She didn't care. More than that, *he* didn't care. "We have to stop meeting like this," she muttered, trying to soothe the two orange tabbies as they both lifted their heads and stared with reproach at this newcomer.

Bryan stepped onto the porch and sent her his trademark crooked grin, the one that did funny things to her stomach in spite of the fact that she'd refused to acknowledge those things.

And not for the first time, she acknowledged somewhere deep down that Bryan was acting far more "mature" than she. Darn him.

"I hope you don't mind," he said. "I looked up your address in the computer."

"I mind."

His lips curved, but he said nothing to that, simply sat on the bench right next to her. "So. What's this about a Christmas curse?"

"It means I have yet to successfully manage a smooth holiday season."

"Ever?"

She didn't, couldn't, answer. Not when their thighs brushed, their arms touched, and his face, when he turned it toward her, was completely void of the laughter she'd been silently groaning over ever since he caught her trying to kiss Matt.

"I'm sorry you had to go through all that," he said, reading her mind with horrifying ease.

"Which? Nearly killing our vice president, or having him now be afraid of me?"

"That you didn't believe me the first time."

"Oh. That."

"Yeah." He nudged her shoulder with his. "*That.* Katie, is it so hard to believe? That you and I could have shared a kiss?"

"It wasn't *just* a kiss."

"No," he agreed with a rueful laugh. "It sure wasn't. And if I hadn't had that ridiculous costume on, if we hadn't been surrounded by dressed up, drunken fools, if…" His eyes gleamed with heat. "Well. Maybe it was for the best."

She was certain somehow his statement should make her feel better. It didn't.

"So…are you going to admit it?"

"Admit what?"

He let out a short laugh and shook his head. "You can't fool me, you know. I'm the master of avoidance techniques."

"You don't avoid anything. You jump into every single day with your eyes wide-open, one-hundred-percent ready for anything and everything. Don't tell me you know anything about avoidance techniques.''

''Ah, but the adventure and excitement of my job, that has nothing to do with what I'm talking about.''

''And what are you talking about?''

''*Heart* stuff. *Emotion* stuff. That's what I'm the master of avoidance at.''

She stared at him, and he stared right back, his eyes clear and open and honest.

''Why?'' she whispered. ''Why are you telling me this?''

''Because maybe I'm a big fake,'' he whispered back. Slowly, as if he were afraid to frighten her off, he lifted a hand. His fingers brushed her cheek in a soft, barely there caress. ''When it comes right down to it, I've never taken the biggest risk of all. I've never opened my heart all the way to a woman.''

''I find that hard to believe.'' Was that her voice, all whispery and light? Good Lord, she sounded as if she were having an attack of the vapors. But then he shifted a little closer and those long fingers cupped her jaw, and she became much more seriously breathing challenged. Her pulse raced. Her heart pounded. Her palms went clammy.

Wait, she *was* having an attack of the vapors!

"You're breathing funny," he said.

Well, so was he. "I thought you loved your care-free lifestyle," she said softly.

"I do. I'm just saying…hell." A self-depre-cating laugh escaped him. "I have no idea what I'm saying."

"I've seen customers fall all over themselves to get your attention," Katie said. "I've seen half the staff—the *female* half, that is—do the same thing. And I certainly haven't seen you running away. In fact, I've *personally* witnessed you opening up one of your planes to at least a dozen different dates."

"I said I've never opened my *heart*. Not my planes, or…anything else."

"Really?"

"Really."

"Why?"

"Why? Because I have enough women in my life with my family. Because I never felt the need for another nosy, bossy—"

"Hey! We're not *all* like that."

"Then maybe I haven't met the right woman."

Oh, she didn't want to know this, she definitely didn't, because something within her softened, melted. Warmed.

Darn it. Darn *him*.

Her insides were going all molten on her, dissolving with each light stroke of his roughened fingers. "Bryan—"

Now those fingers spread wide, as if he needed to touch more of her, and his thumb slid slowly, languidly, over her sensitive lower lip until it quivered open.

His gaze darkened, his mouth opened, too.

"Bryan—"

"Mmm. Love how you say my name. Say it again."

She nearly did, but then realized her eyes were half closed, her body was straining toward his, and she was one touch away from doing what she'd sworn never to do. She could never become attracted to him.

Too late, claimed a little voice, *far too late*.

She not-so-kindly ignored her little voice, because after all, Bryan Morgan was not a forever kind of guy, no matter what he said. She straightened away from him, clicked her mouth closed and glared at him.

So did Tic.

Toc leaped gracefully from her lap and stalked off, clearly bored.

Bryan just waited patiently.

"Stop that."

"Stop what?" he asked innocently.

Making me forget why I don't want you. "Stop waiting for me to tell you what you want to hear."

"Which is?"

"That I kissed *you.*"

He laughed softly, sexily, and her stomach tightened again. *Oh, Lord,* she thought frantically. *It's true.* No more fooling herself, because that's really what she'd been doing.

She'd known the truth all along. It *was* him, no matter how much she wanted to believe otherwise. Worse, she was helplessly attracted to *this* leanly muscled, sleek, sleepy-eyed, sensual man in front of her.

And she'd kissed him.

"Come on, truth now," he said huskily. "You know it wasn't Matt in the Santa costume."

She could only stare at him.

"Let me prove it," he said softly. "I can, you know." His eyes seconded the motion. His mouth curved invitingly, and Katie actually shifted slightly, instinctively moving closer.

"Right here, right now." His gaze was on her mouth. "Let me lay all these doubts to rest for once and for all."

Heat pooled in all the places in her body she'd ignored for so long.

"Katie?" His fingers toyed with her hair. Their mouths were only a fraction apart, but he wasn't moving any closer, he was going to make her ask for it.

Her body was already begging.

"Come on," he whispered, his heavy-lidded eyes dark and sleepy and filled with promises.

So many promises.

But promises weren't good for her, she'd had one too many broken in her past, too many from the likes of a man like this, a man who had no intention of ever settling down.

There. That was the bottom line. She needed to remember that.

Saving herself from making a huge mistake, she jerked back, and in the process startled her cat.

Tic straightened from her lap, meowed softly, then leaped from her legs to Bryan's.

Whether or not the heavy cat missed on purpose—with her claws out—landing directly in the juncture between Bryan's thighs, and the intriguing bulge there, Katie couldn't be sure.

But she had to admit, it was quite a conversation stopper.

"That's two," Bryan said in a choked voice.

"Two?"

"Two men down for the count today." He

groaned and bent over. "That's got to be a personal record for you."

IT TOOK HIM A WHILE, but Bryan finally figured out he'd been going at this Katie thing all wrong. He wasn't usually so slow in the woman department, but to be fair to him, it had been a long time and he was rusty.

Not to mention—Katie was everything he'd *never* wanted. She represented stability, dependability, and…what else was it she'd said?

Oh, yes, reliability.

She probably wanted a white picket fence and two point four kids, too. And yet, he couldn't stop thinking about her, dreaming about her.

It was scary stuff and he vowed to get over it, and quickly.

The morning after nearly getting a vasectomy from Katie's cat, he flew a particularly tough stunt for a commercial—made all the tougher because in spite of himself, his mind kept slipping back to a certain soft-eyed, warm-spirited, strong yet vulnerable Katie Wilkins.

After the flight he sat for a long moment in his plane before pushing himself out of the cockpit. As he turned toward the aircraft's door, it was suddenly filled with a curvy grinning blonde.

"Don't even *think* about it," he muttered to Holly, remembering the last time she'd cornered him in this very spot.

She lifted an innocent brow. "Playing hard to get, Bryan? That's so sexy in a man. And so pointless. Every woman worth her pumps knows with the right…shall we say *motivation*, a man is putty in her hands."

Bryan sighed. "Why don't you give me a break and go ruin some other guy's chances for a change?"

She grinned. "Oh, did I ruin your chances with Katie? What a terrible shame, your actually having to work hard at getting something you want."

It was true. He hadn't had to work at anything, not once in his entire life, because up until now, it had all come easy—school, friends, lovers. *Life.*

Another reason to get over Katie.

"You poor, poor man," she said, tsking softly in her throat. "Trying to get a woman who has no intention of ever falling for a man like you. You're fumbling around in the dark on this one, trust me."

He narrowed his eyes. "Why is that?"

"I could tell you why she's so squirrelly about the attraction between you two, but…nah."

"You owe me one."

"I owe no one."

"I wore that damn Santa costume so that you could trick Katie into making a fool of herself in front of Matt, all so you could make sure he noticed no woman but you."

Holly rolled her eyes and looked bored. "What a convoluted idea *that* would be."

He matched her bored expression. "Of course, I could just tell Matt—"

Her eyes sharpened. "Wait. That…won't be necessary."

He smiled. "I didn't think so. So…spill it."

"You mean let you in on our little Katie's private torments? Tell you that her father was a dare-devil stunt pilot just like you, one who made promise after promise to her that he always broke because a cool and thrilling job would come up? Tell you that after breaking her heart over and over again, he managed to *really* destroy her by getting himself killed on a job he had no business taking in the first place?" She lifted a negligent shoulder. "I suppose I could tell you all that, and all the sad little details that go with it, but… Well, that wouldn't exactly be like me, would it?"

Bryan stared at her, but for once could see no intent to deceive. "Tell me you're lying."

''Would I do that?''

Heart heavy, he closed his eyes and shook his head. *Oh, Katie.*

''Oh, please,'' she said with heartfelt disgust. ''Don't feel sorry for her, she always made out in the end. She and her mother received a huge life insurance settlement. She went to the college of her choice. She got to become whatever she wanted— God knows why she'd waste it on becoming an accountant, but that's another story. Fact is, she came out smelling like a rose.''

''And you didn't,'' he said quietly, finding himself pitying Holly, not Katie. What kind of a woman would look at Katie's life, and what she'd been through, and resent her?

But what he felt for Katie was far more complicated than pity. Compassion, empathy, yes. Definitely all that and more. Also a fierce pride for what she'd done for herself in spite of the obstacles she'd overcome. But there was a new understanding for what she saw when she looked at him.

And it wasn't pretty.

All this time, he'd been allowing himself to get caught up in the bafflement of why a woman with so much hidden passion and love for life would stifle herself. Why she would pretend she didn't feel, and even worse, pretend she didn't need some-one to feel for her in return.

He hadn't considered the possibility her past had driven her to that.

Did she really believe she'd be happy going along with the status quo for the rest of her life, avoiding adventure and excitement, never knowing what she was missing?

Yes, he decided, because she *did* know what she was missing. Hell, she was missing it on purpose so as not to get hurt.

He was outside her office, his hand raised to the doorknob before he knew what he was doing. But her office was empty. He let himself in and stood staring down at her neat-as-a-pin desk, realizing that knowing Katie's past was only half the prob-lem.

The other half was their basic differences.

Nothing was out of place here, not one piece of paper, not a single pencil, not even a paperclip.

Hmm.

Quickly he retraced his steps down the hall, needing to make sure, but—

Yep.

He opened the door to his own office and took in the wild, unorganized mess. Huge piles of paperwork were haphazardly stacked everywhere. Some had fallen over onto other piles, creating bigger mountains. When he'd run out of desk room he'd used floor space, nearly every inch of it.

No doubt. They were indeed opposites.

He attempted to straighten out some of the clutter, but no matter where he shifted a pile, the place still looked like a disaster area. Finally, he opened the large drawers on his desk and just shoved some of the paperwork into them. When they were full to overloading, he coaxed and jammed and threatened, and only slammed his fingers once, maybe twice.

Swearing, sucking on his sore fingers, he went to work on the files all over his floor, but he'd gotten exactly nowhere when he looked up at the shadow in his doorway.

Katie stood there, staring down at him with a bemused look on her face. "Did you lose something?"

He was on his hands and knees, surrounded by a mess he had yet to come close to fixing, even after hours of work. Worse, she didn't look surprised, and that really irritated him. Dammit, he could be neat if he had to. He could!

"No," he said stiffly, and casually kicked a pile

beneath his desk, hoping she didn't notice. "I know exactly where everything is."

"Uh-huh."

He ignored her, and when he looked again, she was gone.

The mess wasn't.

And he was very tired of cleaning.

Maybe, he figured, it was time to regroup. Shift gears.

Attempting to make himself more like Matt was a really bad idea. He didn't *want* to be like Matt. He liked himself just fine, and thought Katie probably did, too. She was just scared.

And with good reason.

He wanted to show her that risk could be good, certainly better than stability and neat desks. The scary part was, he wasn't even sure why it all mattered so terribly much.

Why *she* mattered.

Damn, this was getting complicated. Normally, he was good at complicated. But despite having so many sisters, he didn't really do well as it applied to a woman.

"Definitely need a new plan," he muttered, rubbing a finger along the thick dust on his desk. "A good one."

He mulled over the facts. One, whether she admitted it or not, Katie felt safe and relaxed with Matt. Two, she did not feel safe and relaxed with Bryan. She felt out of control, hot and itchy.

All he had to do was convince her that out of control, hot and itchy was a good thing.

How hard could that be?

7

MATT CAME BACK to work the week before Christmas.

The day he did, Katie hid out in her office, pretending everything was peachy, when of course it wasn't. How could it be? In her quest for Mr. Perfect she'd overlooked one minute detail—*his* feelings.

It went even deeper than that. She'd thought her needs simple—she wanted a nice, secure, happy life with a nice, secure, happy man. Someone who knew his goals and responsibly went after them, someone who didn't let fun run his life.

So why then had her dreams been taken over by a man who didn't fit the criteria, a man who lived his life the same way he flew his airplanes? With wild, reckless, adventurous abandon?

Now Matt was back and she was fairly certain her job was in jeopardy. Her stomach rumbled in spite of having bitten all ten fingernails down to the quick, which was probably a lot more nutritious then her usual breakfast of sugar-coated cereal.

Searching her desk, she came up with three candy bars and happily devoured them all. When she was finished, her skirt felt too tight, but at least the sugar gave her a sense of energy.

Holly poked her head into her office. "My, don't you look...stressed."

Suddenly Katie found a silver lining and managed a smile. "Be nice. This is probably our last day working together." She spared a thought to wonder how much unemployment benefits paid. Or how she'd explain the reason for losing this job. *Well, you see, ma'am, it all started when I gave our vice president a concussion while attempting to sexually harass him.*

Now wouldn't *that* look good on the old résumé.

"Why would this be our last day together?" Holly asked.

"I don't think giving Matt a bump on the head—" not to mention making him paranoid about mistletoe "—is likely to get me a promotion."

Holly laughed and perched a slim hip on the corner of Katie's desk. "You're making way too much of a little accident."

"Uh-huh. Oh, and by the way, thanks for tricking me at the party."

"I don't know what you're talking about. But then, I rarely do."

"I know what you did, and even for you, it was really low."

Matt walked by her office right then, his arms full of paperwork. He didn't so much as peek in. Actually, he sped up, nearly running by.

Holly grinned and looked at Katie. "Guess he's in a hurry." She rose and moved to the door. "Hello, Matt," she called, and Katie winced.

"Don't call him in here!" she whispered in panic, slipping out of her chair and onto her knees behind her desk. She ducked. "I'm not ready for the firing!"

"Well then, don't let him see you." Holly pasted a bright smile on her face as Matt reluctantly came back to the doorway.

"Don't worry," Katie heard her say to Matt in a soothing voice. "The big, bad accountant is gone."

"I thought I saw her...."

Katie crouched farther down and decided the heck with getting fired, she was going to end up in prison. For Holly's murder.

"Oh, she's long gone," Holly said sweetly to Matt, in a voice that said *I'll protect you!*

Katie rolled her eyes as they left together, and wished she had more fingernails to bite.

AT LUNCH Katie took her sandwich and soda outside to watch the planes landing and taking off.

Above her came the drone of an approaching Cessna. The wings gleamed in the sun, reflecting the spectacular blue sky. It swooped in close then soared upward again, the pilot apparently having a ball as he yet again dipped close, this time coming in for his final approach.

As she watched, the wind whipped her face, her hair, and still she just stood there, watching, knowing by the inexplicable tingle in her tummy who it was in the aircraft.

Bryan.

No man had ever given her that tingle before. Certainly not Matt, which, if she was being honest, was what had attracted her to him in the first place.

That tingle scared her to death.

But whether she liked it or not, the truth was very simple. Katie didn't want both Matt and Bryan. She wanted Bryan.

Only Bryan.

She couldn't even say for sure when she'd stopped fooling herself, when she realized that she and Matt would be truly poorly matched. Yes, he was charming and intelligent. He was security and stability personified. Oh, and let's not forget the third *S*. He was safe. But he was safe only because he didn't make Katie's heart leap with excitement.

The plane came in for a perfect landing.

She sighed, in both appreciation for Bryan's skill, and with regret for what would never be. From deep within her came an ache, an old one. Her father had been that skilled, and that uncontrollable. Her mother had loved him anyway.

He'd nearly destroyed her.

Katie had witnessed it firsthand and yet here she stood, wondering, fantasizing… Had she not learned a thing? Did she think Bryan was any different?

She was a fool.

With a loud roar, the plane rocketed by her. At the end of the runway Bryan executed a U-turn and then headed back toward her for the tie-down spot.

He'd seen her.

Katie would swear it by the way her inner tingle spread, liquefying her limbs. She realized she stood rooted to one spot, practically quivering, waiting for the sight of him.

Then he appeared, his hair ruffled, his skin deeply tanned, his eyes covered in aviator glasses that reflected her own wide gaze back to her. He hopped down with ease and grace and looked right at her.

Then he grinned.

She nearly responded in kind, nearly went running toward him, but she managed to restrain herself. Barely.

She was pathetic, melting because of a smile!

Over the loudspeaker on the side of the building, came her page. She turned away, so thankful she nearly tripped over her own two feet.

With not near the same amount of ease and grace Bryan had exhibited getting out of the plane, she escaped back to her reality—work.

HE CAUGHT UP WITH HER.

There were others in the large maintenance hangar; in fact it was fairly crowded, and with three large aircraft in the middle, she couldn't see everyone at once.

But she saw Bryan.

Surely he'd come to talk to one of the mechanics, or even another pilot. Maybe he was simply headed for the pilot's lounge.

He looked right and left, searching, though not for her. That would be silly, pretentious.

Ridiculous.

But then their gazes met. He went utterly still,

then slowly reached up and tugged off his aviator glasses, carelessly hanging them on his collar by one earpiece.

Katie didn't so much as breathe. They hadn't spoken much since he'd been practically unmanned by her cat a week earlier. Up until then, he'd always looked at her with what could only be described as a hungry expression, as if she were a scrumptious dessert and he was a starving man.

But today he looked at her differently. With a good amount of hunger still, yes, but she had a feeling that look just might match her own. There was more though, there was—

"Mmm-mmm good," Holly said over Katie's shoulder, staring at Bryan and licking her chops.

Katie's mood shattered. "What are *you* doing out here?"

"Tracking down a stubborn vice president who forgot to pick up his messages." She smiled at Matt who was a plane length away. He had a stack of files in his hand, his glasses on his nose and his deep-in-work expression on his face, until he caught Holly's smile.

Flustered, he smiled back and…dropped his files.

Katie stared at him. Why was it whenever she saw Holly, Matt wasn't far behind? Or was it whenever she saw Matt, Holly wasn't far behind?

Before she could digest this, a beefy trucker lumbered into the hangar.

"Delivery," the man said gruffly, consulting his clipboard which had seen better days and had a sticker across the top of it that said Bite Me.

Holly gave the man the once-over as she walked toward him. "Sugar, don't you guys usually deliver parts to the *back* of the hangar?"

"Um...yeah." He swallowed hard, clearly rendered an idiot by Holly's wide, welcoming smile. "I don't have parts today, it's a truckload of office supplies. Ordered by—" he referred to his clipboard "—Katie Wilkins."

"A truckload?" Katie frowned. "But I only ordered the usual. Pencils, paper, stuff like that." She'd been distracted lately, sure, but could she have been *that* distracted? She glanced at Bryan, felt her pulse race, and admitted the truth. "It couldn't be more than a box or so," she said with one last hopeful protest.

"Not according to the order slip, lady. You've got an entire truckload of paper here."

Everyone looked out the front window, where the delivery truck had been parked. The back door opened with a loud clang and two more beefy men prepared to unload.

"I don't need that much computer paper," Katie protested.

"You ordered it, lady, not me. And it's not computer paper, it's toilet paper. A truckload of toilet paper."

BY THE END of the day Katie had heard every single toilet paper joke she could take.

Needing...something, she waited until everyone had gone, then made her way to hangar two where the overnight clients had tied down their planes.

The hangar was huge, and since the walls were metal, every little sound echoed. Dark had long ago fallen so she should have been nervous, *would* have been nervous in the past, but for some reason tonight, she wasn't.

She flipped on one low light and stepped inside to be immediately swamped by her senses. The hazy perceptions from the low light, the scent of aviation fuel, the chilly breeze that always raced through because of the high ceilings, she experienced them all.

If anyone could see her right now they'd wonder at her strange urge to come stare into the darkness at airplanes. But she didn't care what anyone thought—a first for her. She simply wanted to please herself, and the heck with all the others.

Another first.

At least five silent planes greeted her, maybe more. She couldn't see into the far stretches of the yawning hangar. They drew her, these sleek, fast aircraft. Strange, given it had been a plane that once upon a time had destroyed her entire life.

But irrational and terrifying as it was, she did indeed harbor a secret passion for airplanes. Bryan had seen that passion in her and that had terrified her too. He'd seen past her guard, had been able to read her so well when no one else ever had.

Scary stuff, indeed.

She realized she stood in front of Bryan's plane, her hand on the metal like a lover's touch as she was gazing up, wondering what it felt like to sit inside, what it felt like to be high in the sky, soaring wild and free without a thought or care.

"It takes both," came a deep, familiar voice behind her, assuring her that she'd spoken out loud. "Thought *and* care."

8

"SORRY," Bryan murmured, looking anything but.

Katie had been so wrapped up in her thoughts she hadn't heard him come up behind her.

His dark gaze settled on hers, full of a whole host of things that made her heart race. "I'd pay big bucks for whatever you're thinking right now," he said.

"Me? I'm just thinking…" *What?* That he was the most startlingly beautiful man she'd ever seen? Most definitely. That she was beginning to be sorry he wasn't the type to settle down? Yep, that too. That she wished with a sudden shocking urge she could kiss him again, without the white beard and fake belly? Oh, yeah. "I'm just thinking it's probably past time I get on home. I—"

Bryan laughed and moved even closer, his broad shoulders blocking out the one low light. "Just thinking about home, huh?"

Yeah. Home. Which had a bed. Which she could imagine Bryan in, the sheets twisted around his naked body. He would have a beautiful physique to match that beautiful face, she thought, and given his personality, and how he attacked life with full gusto, she could only imagine what a fabulous, giving, earthy, uninhibited lover he'd be.

He let out another low, sexy laugh. "You sure that's all?"

"Yes."

"The way you're stroking my plane, Katie, makes me think you're not telling the truth."

With horror, she glanced down at her hand, which was indeed still moving over the side of the plane with slow, methodical, loving strokes. With a small, choked sound, she jerked her hand back, but Bryan took it in his and brought it up to his mouth.

"Tell me," he whispered against her skin.

"M-my thoughts?"

He nodded, and nibbled at her knuckles, then soothed the spot with a soft, surprisingly tender, openmouthed kiss.

She let out a shaky breath, but it ended in an uncontainable moan when his tongue darted out and drew her finger into his mouth, which he slowly sucked while holding her gaze captive in his.

Her knees, which she'd firmly locked at his first touch, turned into jelly.

"Your thoughts," he reminded her.

"Bryan, when you put your hands and mouth on me, I can't think at all."

She'd expected a flare of triumph at that, but he simply closed his eyes, slipped an arm around her waist and dropped his forehead to hers. "So honest," he murmured. "So sweet. I want to taste you, Katie."

Quickly losing touch with her rational side, she searched her brain for something to slow down the moment, to give her some breathing room. "You seem to feel that way right here a lot. I've seen you in action."

"What?"

"Holly. Remember that? Her lips locked on yours? Not to mention her legs wrapped—"

"I remember." He dropped his hand from her side. His eyes went curiously flat. "I didn't kiss Holly."

"No, she kissed you."

"You trust me that much at least."

"I understand there's a difference between kissing and being kissed."

"Do you?" he murmured. "I wonder."

The sudden flicker of amusement in his gaze confused her.

"Come here," he said abruptly, and shouldered open the plane. He tugged her along behind him, until they stood inside.

"I'm going to tell you something I wouldn't admit to anyone else." He lowered his voice as if he were parting with a state secret, his voice husky with mirth. "I've *never* kissed a woman here." He still held her hand tightly, as if he thought she'd bolt at the first opportunity. *"Never."*

"But you've been *kissed* by a woman here. Is that it?"

"As you said, there's a big difference between the two." He leaned back against the wall, put his hands down at his sides, open-palmed against the wall. He should have looked helpless and vulnerable in that position, but he looked about as helpless as a lion out for a hunt. He spread his legs a bit so he and she were the same height, but other than that, he remained perfectly still, not making a move to touch her. "Come here," he said again.

As odd as it seemed, it excited her, seeing all his strength so carefully restrained. "You...want to kiss me?"

"No, I want *you* to kiss *me*."

Her heart nearly parted company with her chest. She managed a laugh, but he didn't so much as crack a smile. His dark eyes were filled with the challenge.

Could she kiss him?

Oh, yes, she could, she most definitely could. Slowly she leaned closer, careful not to touch him with any part of her body, though she had no trouble detecting the sudden tension that seized him when she came within a breath of him.

Heat shimmered through her again at the sense of all his leashed power and passion.

"Kiss me," he whispered.

She did, once, lightly brushing her lips over his. The jolt she felt at the connection shook her to her toes, but she wiped her face clean of expression and leaned back. "There."

"Hmm," he said with a lift of one shoulder.

"Hmm, what?"

"Nothing."

"It's something!" she insisted. "I kissed you, just like you asked." Defiant, her body humming, she did it again, leaned forward and touched their mouths together, only this time she lingered for one second longer, unable to control herself. "See?" she asked a little breathlessly, noticing that his hands were now fisted tightly as if he'd had to hold back from reaching for her.

"What I see is that you're holding back big time." He pushed away from the wall, setting his hands on her shoulders and putting her in the same position he'd just vacated. "Now."

Her stomach clenched. "Now *what?*"

"Now *I'm* going to kiss *you.*"

Panic skittered up Katie's spine because she knew perfectly well she could resist one little kiss, even if her knees were still quaking from the last one, but resisting a *big* kiss, when she knew exactly how thrilling, how hot, how everything, one of Bryan's kisses could be…well, he might as well ask her to jump into Niagara Falls without a life preserver. "I'm not sure this is such a good idea," she said faintly.

His hands had rested on her shoulders. Slowly they slid down her arms to the very tips of her fingers, then back up again, up, up, up, until he cupped her face in his big, warm hands. "It's just the difference between giving the kiss and getting it, remember?"

"Look, I realize you want to show me that *Holly* kissing *you* isn't the same thing as *you* kissing *her,* but—"

"No. I want to show you that Holly kissing me isn't the same thing as what we shared the night of the Christmas party, when we were kissing each other.''

"Oh," she breathed, and though she held herself very still against the wall, just as he'd done, she could feel her entire body pulsating with anticipation.

"You're shaking," he whispered, his hands on her waist now as he gently drew her up against him. "Am I scaring you?"

"No! No, I'm just…" How to put words to what she was feeling inside when she didn't even know herself? "I'm nervous," she admitted.

"Don't be."

"Right." But her voice still wavered with that shimmering, uncontrollable anticipation. "We're just proving a point anyway."

"Uh-huh. A point." His voice was deep, husky, barely audible. *Thrilling.* His mouth hovered near hers, his breath soft and warm on her face.

She wanted to be kissed so badly she nearly met him halfway. *Now,* she thought, *please, now,* but still he just hovered, his gaze steady and intense on hers.

"Bryan…"

"Hmm?"

Do it! Kiss me!

"Yes, Katie?"

"Aren't you going to…?"

"Don't want to rush you," he murmured.

"You're not!"

"Because you're still shaking," he pointed out.

"I'm just ready," she said. "*Really* ready."

"Sure?"

"Yes!"

He came a fraction closer, so close she could feel the heat of his firm yet so soft lips, and she let out a little helpless sound of desire before she could stop herself.

"It's just me," he assured her, mistaking the sound for distress. "And you know me now, Katie, or you're starting to. You know it'll be good."

Yes, she knew that. And yes, she knew she wanted this kiss.

But what she didn't know was if she could trust him, *really* trust him, with her heart, with her needs, with her tender, new, burgeoning emotions.

His hands slid around her, then up and down her spine while, unable to keep herself entirely still as he'd done, her own hands moved over his shoulders to his neck,.

In the end, she lifted her mouth and met him halfway. The kiss started off slow and deep, and her toes curled as desire heated her from the inside out. She welcomed his tongue, and thrilled to his low moan when she opened to him. His grip on her tightened pleasurably, as if he couldn't help himself, and the kiss exploded with sudden urgency.

Again her senses swamped her, this time with the heady scent of an aroused man, the almost overwhelming feel of being sandwiched between Bryan's muscled weight and the even harder wall.

He lifted his head and stared down at her, his chest moving with each ragged breath, his eyes dark and so opaque she could see herself reflected there in the deep, heated depths. "There," he said thickly.

"There...?"

A whisper of a smile crossed his face. "Yeah, there. I know I was trying to prove something, but damned if I can remember what it was. You've scrambled my brain."

"I...really?"

"Most definitely."

"Well then...maybe we could do it again. You know, just until we remember why we're doing this."

"Sounds good." He bent his head.

She wrapped her arms around his wide shoulders,

sank her fingers into his dark hair and hugged him even tighter to her, needing to be as close as she could possibly get. Incapable of holding still, she slid her hips to his. It embarrassed her how they undulated of their own free will, but she couldn't seem to control herself.

At her movement, he made a low sound in the back of his throat and pressed her back against the wall, pinning her there with his body, freeing his hands so that he could slip open the buttons on her blouse. When the silky material parted, he looked down as he slowly slid his hands over her shoulders, taking the material with him. Her breasts were covered by a very plain white bra, but it was thin and her nipples had long ago hardened into tight, hard peaks, thrusting out, begging to be freed, to be touched, kissed.

At the sight of her he made that sound again, then again when he brought his face forward, nuzzling her bra aside. His mouth slid across the soft curve of her breast to a beaded nipple, and he sucked her hard into his mouth.

A buzzing sounded in her ears. Her head fell back against the wall with a loud thud and she gripped fistfuls of his hair to hold him to her. Pleasure was a hot wave that crashed over her from her still tingly lips to her curling toes to the aching spot between her legs.

Then he shifted to the other side and she nearly melted to the floor, *would* have if he hadn't supported her with his arms. "Bryan," she managed to gasp desperately. "I need..."

"I know." He settled himself in the notch of her thighs, pressing a knee between them. The friction of his hard, powerful leg against the spot that was so hot and needy brought her one step closer to the edge, and she opened her eyes, shocked at how close to orgasm she was when he'd only kissed her, had barely yet touched her.

The buzzing she'd heard increased and from a haze of desire she saw Bryan jerk, then heard his soft, frustrated oath. "A plane. Katie, there's a plane coming in."

It wasn't unheard of. Many mornings they'd open Wells Aviation to find one or more planes had landed after hours. Usually the pilots would call a taxi from the payphone and find a hotel for the night.

But sometimes they would sleep in their aircraft.

An aircraft which would be landing right outside this hangar any second, if the sudden roar of the touchdown was any indication.

Bryan shoved his fingers into his hair, then let out a growl. "Look at you." His thumb slid over her mouth, which was still wet. His gaze took in her rumpled state, her obvious confusion, and his frustration dimmed, to be replaced by a tenderness that had her blinking. "Come on, sweetheart." And he reached out to fix her bra, which had the backs of his fingers brushing over her still aching nipples.

Another whimper escaped her before she could stop it and Bryan groaned. "Cover up," he whispered, brushing a kiss over her damp temple.

Cover up? But her hips were still moving, her legs tight and shaking, and she needed—

"Katie," he breathed softly, and he reached for her hands, putting them on her own opened blouse. "Why are you making me be the grown-up?" he asked with a sexy grimace. "Button up, I'll go stall whoever it is."

Button up. Yes, she could do that. But be grown-up about it? She didn't know. Fumbling with the chore, she drew a deep breath and wondered at the insanity of what had just happened.

It was supposed to have been just one kiss.

Simple, right?

Only it'd been anything but, and she had no

doubt, if that plane hadn't just interrupted them, they might have made love.

What had come over her? Unable to believe it, she made her way out of the dim hangar. Actually, staggered was more like it, as if she'd just polished off a glass of wine. *Drunk on lust,* she thought, and let out a laugh that sounded hysterical to her sensitive ears.

At the door, she realized the night had grown cold, icy cold, which she hadn't noticed since she'd been steaming up the air with that kiss.

Kisses, she corrected. Definitely plural kisses.

Bryan was talking to someone. She stepped closer, then was very sorry. Standing in front of her were two of their staff members, both part-time mechanics. With them was Holly, who grinned when Katie showed herself.

"Well, well," she said, her grin widening. "I suppose you were just…what, maybe catching up on some work?"

"Um…" Katie's brain was still fogged with passion. "Yes. Work."

She heard Bryan groan, saw him move toward her, blocking her from view, but she didn't understand why until she heard Holly say, "*Work.* Yes, that explains why you're buttoned wrong."

Katie looked down at herself.

She'd mismatched not one, not two, but *three* buttons. "Oh, boy," she whispered.

Holly just laughed. "Yeah. Oh, boy."

9

ONE DAY LATER Katie found herself craning her neck for a better view of Bryan.

He flew by.

Then again.

And again.

In the long, torturous moments between those appearances, Katie knew exactly what he was doing, even if she couldn't see him.

Stunts.

Dangerous ones.

Upside down, sideways, a roll, he would do them all. And even though she told herself he was free to do as he wanted, that she had no hold on him, and he no hold on her, she still felt like grabbing him right out of the sky and locking him in a safe dungeon somewhere.

She realized she stood at her office window with her nose pressed up against the glass. With effort, she forced herself to relax, even as he finished filming.

She'd known, hadn't she, what he did for the thrill as well as the extra money? Somehow she'd forgotten that basic fact. That it was slammed home now when she stood quivering on the ground while he so foolishly risked his life, didn't improve her temper.

He was so totally wrong for her.

All men had a long list of faults, but Bryan had more than his share. First, he gave her hot looks that fried her brain. Second, he gave her hot kisses that fried her brain. And third, *everything* he did or said fried her brain.

Oh, and he was passionate about everything, including her.

Wait. Those weren't exactly faults, were they?

No problem, she could come up with others. He was startlingly tender and gentle, and he made her laugh at things, at work, at herself.

At life.

Darn. Those weren't faults, either.

How had this happened? He brought out the worst in her. He did! She'd sent an entire truckload of toilet paper to the maintenance hangar, for God's sake.

It had to stop.

She just didn't know how. So she went back to

what had become her own private spectator sport. She plastered her face to her window and watched him fly.

AS WAS HIS PREFERENCE, Bryan tied down his own plane, only this time his mind was not on the job at hand.

He'd nearly lost it up there.

"Ace! That was fab, man, absolutely—"

Bryan lifted a hand to Ritchie to ward him off. He didn't want to talk about his latest stunt, he didn't want to talk at all.

He passed right by the film crew, who were still congratulating themselves on a job well-done, as if *they'd* risked their lives for a stupid beer commercial.

The fact was, Bryan was disgusted with himself. Hell, he was disgusted with the whole world at the moment, and needed to be alone to think.

One wrong move up there and he could have died. It was a thought that had rarely occurred to him before, even on hundreds of previous, more dangerous flights, and yet he couldn't stop thinking about it now as his long stride churned up the tarmac. He entered the lobby and made a beeline for his office.

It wasn't as though his plane had malfunctioned

or failed him. No, it had been his own hands, when he'd held the spin for a fraction of a second too long.

He'd had control at all times, but still, for the first time in his life, he'd imagined the *could have,* the *might have,* the *almost.*

Then imagined himself dead.

And it wasn't his own pain he thought of, but his family's. He was the baby, the joy of his parents' hearts. How would they take it?

And Katie. God, Katie.

It would kill her.

All for a stupid beer commercial.

He passed the women at the front desk, each of whom grinned and sent him the thumb's-up sign.

He passed several clients milling around in the lobby, who wanted to comment on his expert flying.

He passed Holly in the hallway, who managed to annoy him with one easy smile. "Do you make love the way you fly?" she wondered, her eyes laughing. "Because if you do...wow."

Bryan moved faster, needing solitude, needing, for some inexplicable reason, to touch base with his family and hear their voices.

Needing...

He moved by Katie's door, which was ajar. She

stood with her slim, straight back to him, staring out the window at the tarmac.

At his parked plane.

He stopped so fast he nearly tripped.

She'd watched.

"Katie." He'd whispered it before he could stop himself and though she stiffened, she didn't move. "I'm sorry…" Sorry for what exactly? "That you had to see that. That—"

She didn't turn to him. "I've been watching you fly stunts for months, why would you apologize now?"

He wished he could see her face, wished she was in his arms, straining against him as she had last night…he wished for so much he didn't know where to start.

"I'm really busy," she said pointedly, still not looking at him.

"Yes, I can see that."

"Then you'll be sure to shut the door on your way out."

Well. That couldn't be any more clear, could it? No matter that he didn't want to walk away, instead wanted to make her relax, even smile.

He was a man of action though, not of subtlety, and she wasn't ready for action.

Or that's what he told himself as he backed out of her office and shut the door.

Two minutes later he was in his own office with his oldest sister on the telephone, and just the sound of Mandy's voice made him smile.

"What have you done now?" she asked. "You only call me when you're feeling guilty about something."

"I do not."

"Uh-huh. When did you call me last, Bry?"

"Well…"

"Let me refresh your memory. You'd just forgotten Mom's birthday and you wanted *me* to call her up and tell her you'd been held hostage on some remote island."

"Hey, she would have believed it coming from you!"

"And the time before that," she continued, undeterred, warmth and love and affection clear in her voice, "you called because you'd just beat up Cindy's boyfriend and you didn't know how to tell her."

"I didn't beat him up. Exactly."

"I suppose he got that black eye by walking into a door."

Actually, he had. His sister's no-good boyfriend had cheated on her with a close friend. When Bryan had run into him in town, the boyfriend had taken one look at Bryan's furious face and whirled to run, smacking himself on a door so that Bryan didn't have to.

"And don't forget when you crashed Dad's prized '69 GTO into the mailbox because you were busy yelling at me for wearing too much makeup."

Bryan laughed. "I was sixteen."

"And let's not forget our famous trip down the driveway—our steep driveway—on what you so lovingly called a rocketship, but was really just a cardboard box?"

"Hey, my arm healed and you can see almost perfectly out of that right eye!"

She laughed. "And who, in spite of her pain, covered for you?"

At her soft voice, he smiled. "You. Always you." Suddenly he felt better. Warmed somehow. "Thanks, sis."

"For what? Don't you hang up yet, you haven't told me what's—"

"For loving me," he interrupted, because it was the only way to cut her off. She'd talk forever if he let her. "I love you, too."

"Bry! Don't you dare hang up on me—"

Gently, he set the phone down, and when he looked up and saw Katie standing in his doorway, her hands clasped tightly together, nervousness so clear on her lovely face as she offered him a hesitant smile, his heart stuttered.

"You're busy," she said. "I'll just—"

"Stay. Please?" he added, walking toward her.

"You love your family."

"Always."

"They love you back," she said, retreating as he came toward her.

"Mostly," he said with a smile as he cornered her.

"Even when you do crazy stuff."

"Uh-huh." Their bodies brushed. She was breathless, and he was getting there. "That's how family stuff works."

"I was rude before," she said quickly, lifting her hands to his chest when he reached for her. "I wanted to apologize..."

"Katie—"

"I never meant to kick you out like that, but I was watching you fly and—"

"Katie—"

"And it reminded me of—"

"I think about you all the time," he said, dipping his head to slide his cheek over her hair. "Even when I'm flying. You should know that."

"My father—" She stopped abruptly, finally allowing his words to sink in. "What?" she whispered. "What did you just say?"

He stared at her, shocked at himself. "I think about you too much. Tell me about your father."

"No, wait." Katie had put a hand to her heart, absently rubbing there as if she ached. "That thinking about me thing. Why can't you just *stop* thinking about me?"

"I've tried."

"You're not trying hard enough."

"Do you want me to stop?"

"Yes. No. *I don't know!*" Her hands fisted in his shirt, probably to push him away, but she held on. "You're sidetracking me." She stared down at her fingers clutching him, and as if she just realized what she was doing, she loosened them and smoothed over the wrinkles she'd caused. "I came in here to apologize and you're going to make me forget that, or even why."

"Sorry." He had no idea what for, but if she wanted to hug him and apologize, who was he to say no? "Go ahead, beg for my forgiveness."

"For what?" she asked, annoyed.

"I don't know exactly, but I'm certainly going to let you do it."

"Bryan…darn it! You ruffle me."

"You ruffle me, too. Do it some more."

"This is crazy. I can't...do this. Not with you."

"Because of what I do?"

"Because of *who* you are. You remind me of—"

"Your father?" he asked, gently nudging her. "Come on, Katie, open up. Tell me. He hurt you, I know he did, and you never talk about it, it's not healthy. It'll make you explode, or—"

"Or cause me to be unnecessarily rude to you?" She let out a smile. "Too late."

"You haven't been rude, just...a bit prickly."

She laughed at that, then set her head on his chest. "I'm so sorry, Bryan, for so many things."

He didn't need another reason to draw her close, to tuck her body against his and hug her tight. That she let him was a bigger thrill than any flight he'd ever taken. "Come with me."

"Where?"

Bless his sweet and totally untrusting Katie. "If I said to the end of the earth, would you follow me?"

"I'd have to be pretty far gone to do that."

"So, will you?"

She hesitated, then let out a rueful laugh. "Apparently, yes."

Smiling, he led her to hangar three. When he walked up to one of his Cessnas, she held her breath. And when he took her inside, she let the breath out shakily. He strapped her into the copilot seat, sat next to her, put on his sunglasses, and she went more than a little pale.

"Tell me we're just checking out the new leather seats," she said.

"Yep. From twelve thousand feet."

"Oh, my God." She bit her lower lip. She looked as though she tried really hard to contain a sudden rush of excitement, but he knew her now. Yes, she was afraid, but she was also ready to do this.

"Okay?" he asked.

"Oh, sure. I'm great. Really. Couldn't be better." She looked nervously out the window.

"No stunts," he promised, thinking she shouldn't look so appealing, that it shouldn't be so thrilling to be doing this, with her. "Nothing but straight flying, wherever we feel like going."

"Just like that."

"Just like that. Spontaneity, sweetheart. It doesn't have to be dangerous."

Her gaze slid to his mouth and he nearly groaned. "Do that again," he murmured. "And I'll be happy to delay this little fun until I kiss us brainless."

"This is crazy."

"No. This is fun. Simple, easy, good fun. You've not let yourself have enough of it." He got them off the ground gently, took them into the right altitude gently, did everything as gently as he could, and nearly laughed out loud in triumph at the sheer pleasure on her face. "Breathe," he instructed with a smile. "Or you'll pass out."

"Oh!" She laughed a little nervously and drew in her first deep breath. "Yeah, that helps." After a moment she said quietly, "You're much more complicated than I thought."

"Because I can remember to breathe without instructions?"

"No, because..." She turned and looked out the window again, exhilaration and a sort of terrified joy shimmering from her every movement. "It's incredible up here, amazing. I had—" she turned back to him, her eyes full of so many things, incredible things, she took his breath "—I had no idea," she whispered. "You know, how it would be."

"It's good, isn't it?" he whispered back. "Being so high, soaring through the clouds, riding on the wings of air so crisp you can feel it humming through your veins with every breath."

"Yes. Exactly, yes." She swallowed hard and sent him a shaky smile. "I guess it's not such of a stretch to admit I was afraid to give in to this, because then I would have to admit I can understand some of my father's compulsion to do this. He was a stunt pilot.''

"I know," he said gently. "And I'm sorry. But flying doesn't just have to be about wild stunts.''

"No, I can see that now." She tilted her head and studied him. "I think maybe I can see you more clearly now, too.''

At that, their gazes met and held, and Bryan sent her a slow smile that she returned. It warmed him from the inside out.

And terrified him at the same time.

"I'm sorry it took me so long to admit I knew it was you, Bryan," she said.

"Me, what?"

"Beneath the mistletoe.''

At least they were high above the tree line, or he might have crashed. "I'm sorry." He shook his head to clear it. "Could you say that again?''

"I know it was you I kissed." She sent him another shaky grin. "I've known since…probably that night. About time I admit it to you out loud, huh?''

"You wanted it to be Mr. Perfect, I understand that.''

"I'm sorry I let you think that, too." She grimaced. "I let *myself* think it, when the truth is, I really didn't want him at all, I just thought I did. I'm sorry, Bryan, so sorry I made you feel as though you had to change your entire lifestyle in order for us to—''

She went silent while he lay on a bed of pin nails, waiting, waiting, not breathing…still waiting. "In order for us to what?" he asked very softly.

She swiveled in her seat and looked deeply into his eyes. "It doesn't matter. You're not the settling-down type and I accept that. Just as I accept this irrational attraction.''

"Irrational?"

She nodded. "Absolutely.''

"How so?"

"Look, Bryan, let's be honest at least.''

"Always.''

"I loved my father with all my heart. So did my mother, but nothing we could do or say was ever enough to make him happy. He had to get out there, *up* there, had to push the envelope all the time. Had to risk his neck without a thought as to how we'd feel. Always. And then…''

"He died,'' Bryan finished gently. "He left you angry and hurt and afraid of letting yourself enjoy life.''

"Yes. I understand you, Bryan, I understand, but I can't live with it. I hope you can accept that.''

Like hell. "You don't know me very well yet,'' he said mildly.

"I meant what I said. I understand you, but I don't have any no intention of taking that understanding any further."

"Because of your past."

"Yes."

"I'm sorry, but that's just absurd."

"But—"

"But what? All pilots are crazy, wild thrill seekers? *No.* Some of us value our lives greatly, no matter what you think. Some of us plan to be around for another hundred years."

"A hundred?"

He had the sudden and ludicrous picture of himself at 130 years old trying to make love to Katie.

Oh, yeah, no doubt, he could do it. He let out a little laugh and she glared at him.

"What?" she demanded.

He grinned.

"You're thinking of something dirty," she accused. "I know it."

"It was that old-age thing you just laid on me. I was wondering if you'll still want me when we're really ancient."

"I don't want you now!"

"Oh, sweetheart, don't tell a lie I can disprove

with one touch of my mouth to yours. You know you want me, don't you?''

She glared at him as if he were no better than pond scum, which pretty much gave him his answer.

10

IT WAS THE DAY before Christmas and not a creature was stirring.

Except Katie.

She was more than stirring, she was frantic. Somehow she'd fallen woefully behind in all her paperwork, not to mention year end preparations.

Somehow.

She knew exactly how. She'd wasted the past few weeks making an idiot of herself on a regular basis. Then yesterday she'd spent most of the afternoon in the air.

In the air.

It gave her a secret thrill even now. It worried her, how she'd acted. One smile from Bryan and she'd followed him wherever he'd wanted to go.

So much for being the grown-up, mature one.

The airport was hopping with travelers. The staff watched the clock, and for some reason they all looked so darn merry it drove Katie crazy.

"You may not have heard," Julie said halfway through the morning, "but we're about to have one of those happy holidays. Lots of hugs and kissing and making jolly. It's called Christmas. You might have heard of it?"

"Funny."

Julie studied her for a moment. "You need another Christmas party," she decided. "More mistletoe."

When Katie's head whipped up, Julie's eyes were sparkling with amusement. "You could have told me you kissed Santa. I had to hear it through the grapevine. Was it yummy?"

"Who told you?"

"Holly. She said—"

"Don't tell me."

"—that you jumped Santa."

"Oh, my God."

"Did you really try to kiss him *again?* Is that how Matt got a concussion?"

Katie closed her eyes and groaned.

"Cool!" Julie grinned. "You're a goddess among us office women, you know. We're all trying to figure out what we'll use at the Valentine's Day party to kiss whoever we want."

Katie sighed and bore the moment. But as soon as she was alone again, she picked up the phone and dialed her mother. "Hey, Mom. Yes, I'll be there tomorrow night for ham, wouldn't miss it. Oh, and, um, Mom? Why didn't you ever marry again?"

Her mother was silent for a full ten seconds. "Well that's a loaded question."

"I know, I'm sorry," Katie said quickly. "I don't mean to pry, I know Daddy really destroyed your heart—"

"Damn right he did. No one should die that early."

"I meant because he was never there for you."

"What on earth ever gave you that idea?"

"Well—" Katie let out a little laugh "—he was always flying."

"Because that was his passion. But I was his passion, too."

"You…were?"

"I loved him heart and soul, no one else ever came close to giving me what he did." She sighed. "What a beautiful man he was."

Had she really gotten it wrong all these years? How could that be possible? Her mother had accepted her father, faults and all, and had loved him with a fierceness few ever experienced.

Could she do the same?

She said goodbye, and stared at the phone for a

good long time. Finally she rose and headed down the hall toward the soda machine.

She needed caffeine, lots of it, especially if she was going to finish by a decent time. Tomorrow she'd go to her mom's house, maybe they'd even talk more, but tonight she wanted to be home with her pretty little tree, her adoring cats—okay, not exactly *adoring*—and her annual video of *A Christmas Carol.*

She wanted to be alone to think.

Unfortunately Holly was standing at the soda machine, a huge cinnamon bun in one hand, delicious-smelling hot cocoa in the other, a secret smile on her lips.

Katie put in her three quarters, pushed the button for orange soda and eyed her nemesis. "Ruin anyone's life today?"

"Now *that* hurts." But she didn't look insulted. "We could be friends, you know."

Katie laughed. "Yeah. Right. *Friends.*"

"I care about you."

"Don't take this personally, Holly, but I find that really hard to believe."

"Why?"

"Why? Gee, maybe because you're always making a fool out of me?"

"You're still upset about that fiancé thing."

Holly actually stuck out her lower lip in a pout. "I did you a favor. He was a quiet, mousy man."

"So quiet and mousy he dumped me the moment you flashed him some cleavage." Katie had thought it still hurt, but she realized as she said it out loud, nothing happened. No little pang in her heart, no resentment twisted her nerves.

Nothing.

"Well it took more than just a little cleavage—" Holly broke off at Katie's frown and cleared her throat. "The point is, I was just saving you some heartache down the road."

"And what about the Barbie vacation house? When we were six? You told my mother I didn't want it, that I hated it, when it was all I really, *really* wanted. She gave it to *you* instead." God, she couldn't believe that popped out of her mouth.

Holly couldn't believe it, either. "You've been holding a grudge for nearly twenty years? Over a— a *Barbie* house?"

Apparently so. How pathetic. "Never mind."

"No," Holly said slowly. "I think we should talk about this. What else is going on in that mind of yours?"

"The Christmas party."

"Oh, jeez…are you going to harp on that? Get

over it, would you? You ended up in the right man's arms.''

''How can you say that?''

''Bryan Morgan is hot, hunky, smart and funny—not to mention in-your-face magnificent— and he can't keep his eyes or his hands or his mouth off you. I have no idea what you're complaining about.''

Funny thing was, suddenly neither did Katie. But this confrontation needed to be handled, and now that she'd started, she might as well take it to the end and make a total jerk out of herself. ''You didn't know it would work out this way. Why did you encourage me to kiss the wrong Santa? I've been over it and over it, and it doesn't make any sense. Why would you willingly let me kiss Bryan, when you want him for yourself?''

''But I don't want Bryan, I want—'' She broke off, looked down at her roll, then took a large bite.

''You want…who, Holly?''

In a surprisingly open moment, Holly looked at her, her gaze guileless for once. ''Mmhphmm,'' she said around her mouthful.

''Who?''

But Holly just took another large bite, then suddenly tipped her head into flirty mode as her eyes

focused on someone coming down the hallway behind Katie.

Katie glanced over her shoulder, saw Matt, and
winced. He'd been avoiding her, ever since The Incident, as the staff lovingly referred to it.

She whipped around to tell Holly she needed to
hightail it back to work, mostly because she was a
chicken, but Holly had flattened herself next to the
soda machine so that Matt couldn't see her.

Katie's eyes narrowed suspiciously, but before
she could speak, Matt saw her.

The expression of pure terror on his face as he
realized he was alone in the room with her might
have been comical, if Katie had any sense of humor
left about the situation.

"Oh," he said, stopping abruptly. "Hello," he
added, polite to the very end.

Katie wished just once he'd say what was on his
mind, but then again, since what was on his mind
undoubtedly involved her early demise, maybe his
political correctness was good thing.

Katie took a step forward, intending to go around
him and back to her office where she would once
again willingly drown herself in work.

Matt jerked back.

"I'm just going around you."

"Oh." He let out a shaky smile. "Sorry."

At that moment, Holly peeked out and sent Matt a sultry smile. "Hey there, stranger."

Matt looked at Holly. Holly looked at Matt.

The air seemed to thicken.

"Well, this is fun," Katie muttered.

But Matt didn't so much as glance at her. Instead, every ounce of his concentration was on Holly, and how she ate her roll as she slowly walked toward him, making a big production out of licking her fingers clean. "Mmm," she said with a secret smile. "Mmm, good."

Matt's eyes widened, and when Holly did it again, sucking her first finger into her mouth, the poor man nearly fell over in his haste to get closer. He recovered his balance, then walked directly into the wall.

The calm, restrained, quiet Matt blushed wildly, straightened and jammed his hands into his pockets, all the while staring at Holly's mouth.

"You okay?" Holly asked him, her eyes half-closed, smiling sexily. "You hit pretty hard there, maybe I should…kiss it and make it better?"

"I— You— *Well*." Matt closed his stuttering mouth and blushed some more. "If you'd like," he finally said, his voice a little husky.

Holly's smile spread across her face as she

moved toward him. "Where should I start, Mr. Vice President? Where does it hurt the most?"

"Everywhere," Matt said fervently.

Katie couldn't believe it! She knew for a darn fact she'd never come *close* to making Matt lose his composure, and she'd pulled out all the stops! She'd certainly never, ever, seen him flirt, and he was most definitely flirting now. "What's going on?"

Katie didn't realize she'd asked the question out loud until Holly, her gaze still on Matt, said lightly, "You had your Christmas wish, and I have mine."

Holly wanted Matt.

Holly had always wanted Matt.

It had never been about Bryan at all, but making sure Matt had been free for Holly. *"Oh,"* she said, but neither Holly nor Matt spared a glance for her. The two silly fools were staring at each other with stars twinkling in their eyes.

Well…good. They deserved each other. Disgusted, Katie turned away from them and went back to her office, trying to get her mind back on her job, but it was difficult. Seeing the way Matt looked at Holly, and seeing the way Holly looked back, had caused an odd ache inside her.

She still wanted what she'd always wanted, a

nice, happy, cozy future. Only there wasn't one coming.

Given her luck and aptitude for scaring men with mistletoe, there might never be one coming.

Bryan came into her thoughts. Bright, funny and most vexing Bryan. And because she was very human, she wished that she could...that he would... that they might...

She had no idea what was happening to her. They were completely unsuited, she knew this. And yet, she wanted to see him, darn it, irrational as it was. She wanted to see his crooked grin, hear that bone-melting voice. She even wanted to kiss him again.

But—and this might be a blessing in disguise—she had no idea what his itinerary was. Good. To go into the control room and actually check would require her facing how far-gone she was.

She went anyway.

Chet, one of the maintenance crew, was sweeping the empty control room. Casually, she flipped through the flight records searching for Bryan's entry... Ah, there it was—

"Whatcha looking for?"

What was she looking for? "Um...just checking."

"For...?"

For what? Good question. Her sanity, maybe.

"Bryan is already back," Chet said helpfully.

"Sure am," came that deep voice she couldn't stop thinking about.

She whirled and faced him. He wore his pilot's uniform. His aviator sunglasses hung off his collar, and his mouth curved in that welcoming just-for-her smile. "Want to greet me properly?"

"Uh…" Just like that, every single thought flew right out of her head.

Why had she needed to see him? For the life of her, she couldn't remember. She could hardly remember her name.

Bryan laughed softly, and mindless of their audience, tugged her close. Instead of the heated, passionate, wild, out-of-control kiss Katie half expected, he tucked her in tight to his body and simply hugged her. "Missed you, too," he whispered, and nodding to Chet, he led her out of the room.

"I did not miss you," she said, stiffly.

"Okay."

"I didn't."

He turned her to face him. He was grinning, the jerk. "You were looking for my flight plan."

"So?"

"So…you want me." His eyes went hot. "I want you back."

Her resistance deserted her. "Look, Bryan, it's not that simple."

"Yes, it is. Spend tonight with me, Katie. Let's ring in Christmas Day together."

"That's for New Year's. The ringing."

"Okay, we can do it again next week. Say yes. Let's banish your Christmas curse and have a great time while doing it."

"You mean sleep together."

"I didn't say anything about sleeping," he said wickedly.

"Bryan."

His fingers lifted to caress her cheek, his gaze softened. "You're nervous. I won't hurt you, Katie."

But he would. He could. "I can't."

"Yes, you can. Come on, it'll make Christmas morning special."

"I...don't have a present for you," she said lamely. As if that was her only concern! She had a million of them! "I can't think of anything in the world you could want that you don't already have."

His eyes darkened, and for a moment she thought he was going to say *you*.

How silly that would be. This man could have anyone, anyone at all.

"No presents," he said quietly. "No pressure. Just you and me."

"Bryan—"

The intercom buzzed. Katie was needed at the front desk for a "disturbance."

Saved by the bell from her own hormones.

Bryan followed her.

Two of their biggest clients waited for her, Rocky and Teddy. They'd been both best friends and enemies for nearly sixty years. Short, chunky and balding, with matching deep squint lines from long days in the cockpit, not to mention identical perpetual scowls, they could have been twins separated at birth, except for the fact that Rocky had lily-white skin and Teddy was African American.

They never agreed on anything, unless it was how much they detested everyone else. Both of them held envelopes and glared at her as she came closer.

"Merry Christmas Eve, gentlemen," she said. "Is there a problem?"

"You betcha, little girl," Rocky grumbled, waving his envelope, which Katie recognized as the monthly statement she'd recently sent out in the mail. "You charged me the going rate for fuel last month."

She didn't understand the problem until Teddy

grinned. "I got the favored customer discount."
His amusement dissolved as he, too, waved his bill.
"But I got charged full price for tie-down fees, and
missy, I *never* get charged full price."

"I didn't get charged full price there." Rocky
beamed. "Because *I* got your preferred customer
discount."

"You—" Teddy's face turned beet red as he
grabbed for Rocky's bill, but Rocky lifted it high
over his head, chortling as the portly Teddy leaped
up and down like a bullfrog, trying to grab it.
Rocky wheezed with amusement, coughing from
his forty year old cigar habit as if he intended to
lose a lung.

Bryan grinned at the spectacle, and when Katie
glared at him, he only laughed. "They'll get it out
of their systems in a minute," he told her. "Once
they get in a good punch or two. Happens all the
time."

"Well, I can't let them duke it out here," she
said firmly, thinking of insurance premiums and
lawsuits.

"Katie—"

"I can handle this."

"But—"

"Let me do my job," she insisted. "Gentlemen!" When they didn't appear to hear her, she

reached over the counter for the envelopes, which were being waved by two greedy fists, high over the men's heads as they danced up and down trying to outmaneuver each other.

"Katie, I could just—"

"No," she said to Bryan over her shoulder. "Believe it or not, I can take care of this on my own."

"I realize that, but if you'd just—"

"Please." Envisioning two heart attacks, or even a stroke or two, Katie reached out farther, but the counter hampered her. Teddy and Rocky weren't just grabbing for their bills now, but actually starting to wrestle, and picturing the calamity when one of them clobbered the other, she became all the more alarmed. "Come on now, let's settle this reasonably—"

That's when Teddy slid in low and punched. Rocky evaded, and in a comical twist that rivaled any raunchy television wrestling show, Teddy swiveled with the follow-through that ended up going nowhere. He fell on his butt on the lobby floor. With an enraged bellow, he went for Rocky's feet, wrapping his pudgy arms around them just as Katie leaned all the way over the counter and grabbed both envelopes. Her toes left the floor, making her gasp at the loss of balance.

She felt Bryan grab her legs, heard his worried voice calling her name.

But naturally, as this day was not one of her best, she overcompensated for her leap up. And as the laws of physics state, what goes up, must come down.

So it was only a matter of a second or so after Rocky tumbled to the floor in a heap over Teddy that Katie lost the battle for balance.

She would have toppled headfirst over the side of the counter, except that Bryan held her legs.

So actually, the only thing that fell was her skirt.

Right around her ears.

As she hung there, held by Bryan, his arms around her thighs, his face only an inch from her proffered tush, her plain white serviceable underwear flashing him, she was fairly certain that nothing else could possible go wrong for the rest of the day.

Naturally, she was wrong about that, too.

Because that was the exact moment that Holly and Matt made their reappearance. No one seemed to notice that Holly's lips were pleasantly swollen, or that Matt had untucked his shirt to cover the front of his pants.

Why should they, when the upside down, dress-flapping-in-the-breeze Katie easily stole the show?

11

BRYAN SHOULD HAVE followed his heart's desire. He should have taken a bite out of Katie's tight, curvy and oh-so-temptingly close rear end.

But he hadn't, he'd actually followed society's unspoken rule—do not bite a lady's bottom unless invited to do so.

And now he was alone on Christmas morning.

Christmas mornings were typically pretty darn good for him. They had been all his life. For one thing, he was the baby of a very large family who believed in lots of love and laughter.

And lots of presents.

Because he wasn't the most organized of men, he sat on his bed and wrapped the things he'd purchased for everyone. Better late than never, he figured with a smile as he unrolled some festive paper and dug in.

He wasn't getting together with his family until dinner, which was good. He wanted to see Katie first.

The nerves surprised him, but as soon as he finished wrapping, he showered, dressed and got into his car.

Getting to her place took no time at all, but he wasted another moment in rare angst, staring at the dark windows and wondering what the hell he thought he was doing. She'd made it clear over and over again he wasn't what she wanted in a man. Not that it mattered; he didn't want to be any one woman's man anyway.

He really didn't.

So why was he here, sitting in his car staring at her house like a fool?

Because he *was* a fool.

Was she even there?

Last night he'd been hoping they'd leave work together, maybe have dinner, and indeed spend Christmas Eve together, just the two of them, but those hopes had gone up in flames at Katie's vanishing act.

She hadn't answered her phone, and he wondered now if she'd skipped town. He knew so little about her, really, and yet he felt her knew her so well.

How could that be?

And even more startling was how much he wanted to spend time with her. Wanted to talk, wanted to share stuff, wanted to hear *her* share stuff. He wanted to laugh with her, wanted to make her laugh. Wanted to just...*be* with her.

And yet she was doing her damnedest to make sure it didn't happen.

Drawing a deep breath, he got out of his car and knocked on her door. From inside came an unmistakable meow, and he relaxed, knowing Katie wouldn't leave town with her cats alone in the house.

A few seconds later he could tell she was looking out her peephole. "Hello," he said to the still-closed front door. "Merry Christmas, Katie."

The door remained firmly shut, and he set his palms on the wood as if he could feel her right through it. "Katie? Let me in. It's—it's cold out here," he improvised quickly, setting his forehead against the wood now, needing to be close to her. "You wouldn't let a man stand out here and freeze to death, would you?"

"Go home, Bryan."

An apology, he decided brilliantly, staring at the door. Women liked apologies. "Katie? I'm really sorry."

A rueful laugh escaped her at his soulful tone. "What are you apologizing for?"

"Um...being a man?"

"I'm not mad at you," she said through the door.

"I'm just—" he heard a clunk and knew she'd set her head against the wood "—just feeling stupid here."

He had to press his ear up to the wood to hear her. "Why?"

"See! This is just what I mean! It'll seem really silly to a man who's never doubted himself for a single second."

"I've doubted myself plenty."

"Uh-huh. Over what?"

"You," he said bluntly. "Over you."

"I'm just one of too many women."

"That's pretty much my point."

Another short laugh. "Was that supposed to make me feel better?"

"What I mean is, this has never happened before."

"What hasn't?"

"I can't walk away. I can't stop thinking about you. I dream about you, ache for you. I need you, Katie."

"You...need me?"

"Open the door and let me show you." At her silence, he sighed. "Please? I have a present." Another trick learned from his sisters, all of whom could be bribed. There wasn't a woman alive who could resist a present.

Except this woman, apparently.

"You said no presents," she said accusingly.

"Open the door, Katie."

She cracked it. "Why?" she asked warily, one cautious eye greeting him.

"Could you maybe open it just a bit more?"

"Well...okay. Just for a— *Hey!*" she cried when he used his superior strength to let himself in.

"Sorry," he said, anything but as he gazed down at her. She was rumpled, her hair wildly rioting about her sleep-flushed face. She wore a pale-rose bathrobe that swallowed her up. Two bare feet poked out beneath the full hem.

He loved bare feet.

"This is crazy," he said, wanting to devour her sleepy, mussed self on the spot. "Tell me what's wrong."

"You mean besides everything?"

"Well...yes."

She looked heavenward, then studied her feet.

"Katie?"

She rolled her eyes. "It's about yesterday."

"I figured out that much."

"You're going to make me say it specifically?"

"Well, since I'm clueless, yes. You'll have to say it. Specifically."

"Okay. You saw...my panties."

He stared at her, wanting to laugh, needing to laugh, but at the glare on her precious face he didn't quite dare. ''Well, since I've been wanting to see your panties for some time, preferably on the floor, on the door handle, on the ceiling fan, anywhere but on you, I can't apologize.''

Her mouth opened, as if she had to do that to breathe. He took the opportunity to reach for her, haul her close and put his mouth to hers. To help her breathe, of course.

She let out a little sound, which he swallowed. Then she grabbed fistfuls of his shirt. He liked when she did that, a lot, but this time she happened to get a few chest hairs in with the material of his shirt and he was surprised at how much a few little hairs, slowly pulled out of his skin, could burn like fire. ''Uh...Katie?''

''Mmm.'' She buried her face in the spot between his shoulder and neck, and he decided he liked that, too, so much he could live with the fire in his chest.

For her, he'd do anything.

Which pretty much terrified him now that he thought about it. ''It wasn't the panty thing,'' he whispered, holding her as tight as he could. ''Admit it. You're just scared. Hell, so am I.''

''I don't like being scared.''

That made two of them. Not knowing what else
to do, he kissed her again, a hot, wet kiss that had
them both breaking off, panting for air.

"Where's my present, Bryan?"

Uh-oh. Damn, he should have known better.
"Um...close your eyes." When she did, he reached
inside his pocket for a scrap of red ribbon from
wrapping his family's gifts. He'd intended to let her
cats have it. "Okay," he said after a moment.

Katie opened her eyes and took in the red ribbon
tied in a crooked bow around his neck.

He sent her a crooked smile to match it.

"*You're* my present?" she asked, her voice soft
and hesitant.

"Don't tell me you want to return it. I didn't save
the receipt. Plus, I bought me on sale, so—"

"Is it for keeps?"

Oh, boy.

"Never mind," she whispered, covering his
mouth with her fingers so he couldn't deny,
couldn't sooth away that slightly stricken, embarrassed light in her eyes. "I don't want for keeps,
either." Then she replaced her fingers with her
mouth.

Katie kissed him hard, her heart squeezing so
tight she thought it was a miracle she could kiss at
all. She'd take what she could get with him and be

okay with it. She'd be more than okay. She'd thought she'd never get over her humiliation from yesterday, but somehow he'd done it, he'd made everything okay, just as he had from the moment she'd made her Christmas party mistake.

Only maybe it hadn't been a mistake at all. "Keep kissing me," she murmured, and the words were barely out of her mouth before his head descended again. He kissed her over and over, until they were panting, straining against each other. He ran his hands down her back to her bottom. With a hoarse murmur, he drew her to him, burying his face in her hair.

"I can't feel anything but warm woman under this robe," he said, his voice so hoarse it was nearly gone.

"I was just about to get into the shower," she admitted.

He groaned, and with characteristic bluntness, opened her robe. Never reserved or shy, he bent his head and looked at her, his eyes so hot she was surprised she could stand so close and not get burned.

A flash of doubt hit her, because it had been a very, very long time for her, and because she'd never felt particularly comfortable in her own skin. "I'm sorry," she whispered, feeling his sudden

stillness like a weight. "I'm not— My body isn't—
I really hate to exercise," she finished lamely.

His unfocused gaze met hers. "What?"

"I'm not exactly…you know, perfect."

His eyes blinked and focused. "Are you trying
to tell me you feel the need to apologize for this
body?"

"Well…" Miserable, she nodded.

"You're kidding me."

"No. My tummy isn't flat." He touched it and
her breath faltered. "And my breasts…they're not
exactly…perky."

He switched his attention to them now and she
could hardly speak. "And my hips…"

"Your hips?" he encouraged, but she didn't
want to even go there.

"Forget it," she muttered.

"Never." He studied her, apparently not in the
least disturbed by her curvy figure because he made
a low, rough sound in the back of his throat, almost
a growl, and hauled her close. "Perfect," he murmured. "Soft, round, sweet and perfect. You're
beautiful, Katie."

"But—"

"But you do talk too much," he decided sinking
to his knees and taking a love bite out of her belly
before he dipped even lower, effectively shutting

her up. Without another word, he opened his mouth on her. His hands, splayed wide over her bare bottom, drew her closer, then closer still as he nibbled, sucked and licked her halfway to heaven.

Unable to help herself, she cried out, because what he was doing to her simply caught her on fire. She had started to shake the moment he put his mouth on her. When she could no longer stand, he simply scooped her up and, following her breathless directions, took her to her bedroom. He set her down on the bed, but not before he spread her robe wide, gently tugging it away.

Morning light streamed in the windows, streamed over her nude body, but the last of her doubts faded in the light of his naked and fierce desire. Then he began to undress and she forgot all about herself. His shirt fell to the floor, revealing wide shoulders molded to a broad, muscular chest. Desperately ridding himself of clothes as fast as he could, his jeans hit the floor. His belly was flat, his thighs powerful. Between them he was heavy and hard.

"Oh, my," she whispered, staring, and he let out a groaning laugh. "Bryan, that's not going to— You're not going to be able to—"

"Fit? Oh, yes I am." He crawled onto the bed and reached for her, running his hands over her breasts, her stomach, her thighs and in between, all the while murmuring husky, sexy, earthy promises that mixed with his greedy and oh-so-talented fingers, arousing her to the point of no return.

He kneeled between her legs, his eyes hot and hungry, watching her closely as he put on a condom. He touched her then, making her cry out his name. He said her name, too, on a tight breath as his fingers slid over her hot, glistening center, and then opened her legs farther and entered her. "See?" he whispered roughly, covering her with his deliciously heavy body. "I fit."

Perfectly.

And then he started to move.

Instantaneous combustion.

It had never happened to her before, immediate orgasm, but it happened now. Endless ripples of pleasure rolled over her body, and her mind continued to reel as he thrust into her again. Then again. Time stopped as he raced toward his completion, and she raced right along with him.

VAGUELY SHE REALIZED Bryan had braced himself above her, his arms trembling violently in the aftermath, his whole body trembling, breathing as harshly as she.

As if to savor the last of his pleasure, he pressed his hips to hers. A low sound escaped him, one that somehow conveyed all she was feeling, and answering it, she reached up for him just as he reached down for her. She pressed her face to the base of his throat, where his pulse still raced.

One big hand came up to cup her head and he held her close. "I had to come," he whispered.

She smiled against his skin. "So did I. And we could always do it again, right?"

He went utterly still, then laughed. "I meant I had to come *see you.*"

"Oh."

He snagged her tight when she would have rolled away in embarrassment. "I like your idea of doing it again," he said with a grin. "I like it a lot." His hands slid over her body, holding her hips still so that he could rock against her.

He was already hard, making her hum in helpless pleasure as his fingers came around and slid between her legs. "Yeah," he said in a rough whisper, finding her hot and wet. "Definitely again." Before she could say anything, he lifted her up to straddle him, and in one powerful stroke buried himself deep inside her. "Ahhh." His eyes opened, held hers. "I felt lost this morning. Until you opened your door, that is."

She could hardly think. It took every bit of energy to open her eyes on his.

"I've found what I was missing," he whispered.

"Me?"

"You." He arched up, filled her even more, and she had the terrifying feeling that maybe she'd found what *she* had been missing, too.

THE DAY AFTER Christmas at any airport tended to be a wild one. It was no different at Wells Aviation. Planes coming and going, office staff trying to deal with end-of-year stuff, people milling everywhere, mechanics running like crazy, half-dazed in their after-Christmas glow, sluggish from overeating and overdrinking and not enough sleep.

Bryan felt half-dazed, too, but it had little to do with overeating and everything to do with not enough sleeping.

He'd been with Katie instead.

Thinking about it now had a foolish and idiotic grin on his face. Actually, the grin had been there for a full day now, and he couldn't swipe it away.

Nothing could.

Had he actually…fallen in love?

Okay, *that* took away his grin. Easily.

It couldn't be true. Yes, he cared about her, greatly, but…love?

God, no. How wrong that would be.

But what if she thought herself in love with him?

No. That would be impossible, too. She couldn't love him. He was unsuitable for that kind of relationship. He didn't know how to do love, and not for anything would he hurt her.

But what if she didn't realize that?

He'd just tell her so. Only she wasn't in her office. She wasn't in the lobby, or in anyone else's office, or on the tarmac.

Damn. By now, he had a plane full of passengers, ready for his chartered flight to San Diego.

''Check the mechanic's hangar,'' Holly suggested, when she came upon him standing forlornly in the lobby.

''How do you know who I'm looking for?''

''Oh, please,'' she said with heartfelt disgust. ''It's all over your face.''

He left for the maintenance hangar at a fast clip.

Holly followed.

''Don't you have work?'' he asked, annoyed.

''Uh-huh.''

After another fifty yards he tried again. ''It's pretty chilly out here.''

''I'm fine.''

Exasperated, he turned to her. ''Look, I don't know why you interfered in the first place, but I really think I can take over my life from here.''

''Well, being a man, you would think so.'' Holly

smiled serenely. "And as much as I'd like to take credit for that stupid grin you've been wearing on your face all day, I should tell you, I did it for purely selfish reasons."

"So why don't you go away for selfish reasons?"

"What? And miss the fun?"

"How do you know I'm heading for fun?"

"I didn't say *you,* big guy, I said *me. I'm* heading for fun. And you're it."

Bryan sighed.

The hangar was opened to the chilly day on both sides. Wind whipped noisily through. No less than four planes were tied down, being worked on by their team of mechanics. Power tools whizzed and whirled, accompanied by the steady drumming beat of a hammer, a compressor and the buzz of men shouting to be heard over all the ruckus.

He saw Katie immediately, and moved toward her. She couldn't have heard him approaching with all the din, and since she was turned away from him, she couldn't have seen him enter, either.

And yet, as if she felt him, she looked up. Across noise and clutter their gazes met, and a smile curved her lips.

Bryan went all warm and fuzzy.

Wait a minute! *Warm and fuzzy?* What was wrong with this picture?

Everything!

Dammit, he was here to tell her not to look at him like that. That if she thought she was in love with him she should just think again. That she should have stuck with Mr. Perfect…

No. God, no. He didn't want that, either.

Confusion was totally unwelcome, and he made the mistake of looking at her again.

She held a clipboard. There was a pencil in her teeth and another behind her ear. She wore a modest navy-blue business suit that had her looking mightily professional, and so adorable his fingers itched to grab her.

His heart squeezed and his confusion tripled, and of their own accord, his feet took him to her.

Gently he tugged on a lock of her carefully restrained hair. "So put together." He had to shout to be heard over the roar around them.

Katie blushed, clearly remembering how only the day before she'd been sporting a radically different look. Hair wild, completely naked, she'd straddled his equally naked body as she'd driven them both to ecstasy.

With not a blush in sight.

"I need to talk to you," he shouted, frustrated at

the noise. "Can we…" He gestured outside, but she shook her head.

"I'm stuck here for a while," she yelled in his ear. "Invoicing."

And he had a plane full of people waiting on him. "But I—"

Another compressor joined the first. More hammering. And a new whine of a power tool upped the volume to beyond loud.

"Yes?" She smiled at him, an angelic, sexy smile in complete contrast with their annoying, overwhelming surroundings.

Tell her. "I…" *Tell her now, that her first instincts were right, he wasn't Mr. Perfect, and never would be. He wasn't a man she could bank on, didn't want to be a man she could bank on.*

"Bryan?" she yelled.

Oh, that sweet smile. "I…"

"You…" she shouted encouragingly.

"Katie…I…" Damn. *"I love you,"* he yelled at the top of his lungs, just as by a twist of fate, maybe his own Christmas curse, the compressors and all the banging abruptly stopped.

So did his heart as those three huge terrifying words rang out in the silent, stunned, amused, *filled* hangar.

Applause rang out. So did whistles and catcalls.

"Woo-hoo!"

"You go, boy!"

"Bryan and Katie sitting in a tree," sang a group of mechanics. *"K-I-S-S-I-N-G!"*

Bryan stood there, rooted by shock.

He dared a peek at Katie, prepared to face her laughter, as well. But she wasn't laughing, she was staring at him, agog, as if she'd swallowed a toad.

Given the blockage in his own windpipe, he knew the feeling.

"You…what?" she whispered.

Oh, sure, *now* they could whisper. "Nothing," he said quickly. "I didn't say anything."

She didn't believe him, of course. And then she walked away, and with each step she took, his poor overwrought heart constricted.

12

WHEN KATIE TURNED on her heel and walked across the hangar toward the only chair she could see, she wasn't exactly thinking. She couldn't. The ringing in her ears and the pounding of her pulse took over.

Driven by a need to sit before she fell, she sank to the seat and closed her eyes.

"Katie."

He had the most wonderful voice, it should be illegal to have a voice like that. He also had the most wonderful scent, a warm, sexy male sort of scent.

That should be illegal, too.

"Hey! Are there going to be wedding bells?" one of the men called out. "Because I think we could do the wedding right here, right in the hangar."

"Yeah! We could part the planes to make an aisle," someone else called out.

"And we could throw O-rings instead of rice!" came yet another brilliant suggestion.

"Touching," Holly said. "Every girl's dream, right Katie?"

Bryan groaned, and Katie opened her eyes. Yep, his expression matched the misery in his voice.

Because of their audience, she wondered, or because he'd blurted out something he hadn't meant to?

Both, most likely.

The intercom system crackled again, making Katie jump. Mrs. Giddeon's voice echoed through the hangar, calling for Bryan to come charter his flight.

Clearly annoyed enough to forget they had clients and passengers listening, the woman threatened to personally hunt Bryan down if he didn't get his "fine-looking behind" to the front, and pronto.

"Would you look at that timing," Holly said with a tsk. "Can't leave passengers waiting, and you certainly wouldn't want Mrs. Giddeon hunting you down. No telling what she'd do to that 'fine-looking behind.'"

"I'm sorry," Bryan mouthed to Katie.

"No biggie," she said, shrugging, as if men mistakenly told her they loved her all the time.

Hey, she'd at least have a memory to keep her warm at night.

"No biggie?" he repeated, looking upset. "I—"

"Bryan," droned Mrs. Giddeon. Unhappily. "You have a mutiny brewing here."

"You'd better go," Katie said.

"But—"

"Oh, please," Holly moaned. "It's just a flight. You'll be separated for what? Maybe four hours? Cripes, children, hold it together, would you? Some of us would like to keep our breakfast down."

Then he was gone, and Katie was still sitting. *Had* to be sitting, since her watery legs refused to hold her. Around her the staff fell blessedly silent. Out of respect, she figured, grateful.

That's when she was hit with a shower of O-rings.

Arms slung around each other, her so-called friends and staff came forward humming—off-key—the wedding march song.

"I SUPPOSE you're going to pretend you don't want to talk about it," Julie said sometime later.

Katie feigned disinterest. *"It* being…what?"

"Helllooo…this morning's declaration? By the wild and hereto uncommitted Bryan Morgan?"

"Oh, *that* it."

Julie grinned. "How totally romantic was that! He declared his love in front of everyone."

"Yeah. Romantic." She was still pulling O-rings

out of her hair. Obviously no one had heard him
tell her he'd said nothing.

"Come on," Julie encouraged. "Tell me how
Mr. Risk came to announce his love for Ms. Security."

Was she *that* easy to read? And anyway, it was
no longer a matter of risk versus security. Yes,
she'd probably always hesitate before taking a risk,
but suddenly—or maybe not so suddenly at all—
she didn't want to settle for status quo, either.

Bryan had claimed to love her.

Good Lord, the most wonderful, exciting, thrilling, fascinating man on the planet had thought for
that one brief shining moment that he *loved* her.

Julie grinned because she'd spoken out loud.
"And now back to our regularly scheduled pro-
gramming, which apparently you're just tuning
into. Do you love him back?"

Oh, yeah. "No."

Julie grinned. "Your dreamy smile answered differently."

"It's lust, not love," Katie said, frowning down
at her clenched hands. She'd seen the horror on
Bryan's face, she knew he wished the words back.
"Lust."

"Well, either one of them works as a hell of a
bed partner on a cold winter night."

Maybe. For a while anyway. But lust wasn't ever going to be enough for Katie, there had to be more.

Bryan was what he was. She knew and accepted that. Maybe he wasn't flying stunts at the moment, but he would be soon, and that was scary, but okay. His sense of wonder at life, his love of excitement and adventure, it had all led her to this point. For that alone she loved him.

And he must never know.

She'd learned a lot about herself in these past weeks. She'd learned that being grown-up and mature is fine, but there had to be room for fun, too, that fun was okay. She'd certainly learned that maybe risk is part of what makes life so worthwhile.

Loving Bryan was certainly the mother of all risks. But she'd get over it. Maybe even try again someday.

And yet…she had the need to prove to herself that she wouldn't lose her nerve, that she would indeed risk again.

In light of that, filled with determination, she marched into the mechanic's hangar. After all, it didn't have to be her *heart* she put on the line, right?

At the sight of her, everything and everyone went

momentarily silent. "No show this time, guys," she announced.

"Bryan loves Katie, Bryan loves Katie," came a singsong voice from the back of the hangar, and trying to maintain her calm, she headed toward it, knowing it was Steve, their head mechanic and also part-time flight instructor.

"Unfortunately," she said in the face of his wide grin. "It's *you* I want to talk to. I want flying lessons." Behind her, everyone gasped.

Katie ignored them. This was *her* risk and she was sticking to it.

Because, really, Bryan had nailed it. All her life she'd been both fascinated and terrified by planes. Getting a job in an airport, however small, had been a step in the right direction. Learning to let a man like Bryan into her life had been another. "I want to start right now," she said quickly, before she lost her nerve. "You have a problem with that?"

"No, ma'am." He grinned. "Does Bryan know you're doing this? Because he might want to be the one to teach you…"

"Can you go right now or not?" She was in a huge hurry to do this now, to prove to herself she could. Without Bryan.

"Well…" Steve took off his hat and scratched his head.

"I'll pay double the going rate," she said rashly, and Steve lifted his brow, nodded and off they went. Just like that, with everyone left gaping in her dust.

Beat that, Katie thought with giddy wonder. It felt great. Better than great. It was almost as good as—

No, nothing was as good as making love, not now that she had Bryan to use as a scale.

But this was indeed a close second.

BRYAN HADN'T EVEN set his feet onto the ground when Julie came flying out onto the tarmac, her shirt flying up to alarming heights in the sharp wind.

"You're not going to believe this," she said, huffing and puffing. "But—"

A plane buzzed them, and Bryan scowled. "*Idiot.* That was too damn close."

"Yeah, about that—"

"Hey." His frown deepened as he gazed upward, shielding his eyes from the sun with his hand. "That's Steve's plane. Is he teaching some idiot to fly like that?"

"Maybe you should come with me," Julie suggested with a tight smile. "To the control room."

"Why?"

"Because that idiot? It's Katie."

BRYAN PACED the small control room like a caged tiger. He alternatively swore at the controls, swore at the sky, swore at the plane as it occasionally came into his view.

All the while Holly, who apparently had nothing to do except torture him, laughed, unperturbed when he turned on her with fire in his eyes.

"Oh, relax, *ace*. She's only taking a flying lesson."

"Yeah."

"And anyway, you probably have work to do." She smiled. "Why don't you vacate?"

He wasn't going anywhere until Katie was down.

"You're sweating, Bryan."

"Holly?"

"Hmm?"

"Shut up."

She only grinned. "Don't you see the irony of this? All these years you've been flying with reckless abandon, never worrying about what it did to the people who care about you."

Bryan stared at her. God. How could she be so right? "Well, waiting really stinks."

"Bingo." And she softened. "You know, who-

ever said *all* men are stupid wasn't quite accurate.
You're not stupid, just slow.''

Bryan shook his head and grabbed the radio
headset. "Katie," he barked. "Come down. Now."

"That's not proper radio protocol," Holly
pointed out.

As if he cared. "Please," he added into the headset while Holly just laughed at him.

KATIE WAS HAVING the time of her life when
Bryan's command came over the radio. She leaned
back from where she'd had her nose pressed to the
window, practically giddy with the thrill, and
looked at Steve.

"Was that...a command?" she asked, shocked.
"Was he *commanding* me to come back down?"

"I don't think a command includes the word
please."

"He *demanded,* Steve."

"But he said please. I heard him."

She'd heard something else, too—an inexplicable
quaver in that deep, familiar voice, one that instincts told her was fear.

For her.

"Steve, would you say I did well for my first
lesson?"

"Well..."

"Okay, forget about that little tower problem on the takeoff."

"We nearly hit it. Twice," Steve reminded her. "I wouldn't call that a *little* problem."

"Other than that, how did I do?"

Steve's lips quirked. "I suppose I should forget about that little dipping problem, as well."

"Hey, nothing wrong with a little roll."

"On your first lesson?"

Katie couldn't help it, she laughed. She felt so incredible, so excited, and she was flying. *Flying.* Up in the air, with the wind beneath her wings, and loving every second.

"Katie." It was Bryan again. *"Now."*

She borrowed the headset from Steve. "No," she said succinctly.

"We need to talk," Bryan said in his sternest voice.

She wasn't sure she liked his tone. "I don't think so."

"Yes, we do. Now, as a matter of fact."

Katie sighed. "Look, you said something you didn't mean. You said sorry. I accepted. If *I* can get over it, so can you."

Total radio silence.

Then he spoke again, his voice not nearly as calm, "Come down, now."

"You know, Katie, I really like you," Steve said. "But I really, *really* like living, so..."

"Bryan wouldn't hurt you! Well, probably not," she amended.

"Steve." Bryan again. Voice carefully controlled. Very tense. "Get her down here or—"

Steve flicked off the radio, but shot Katie a reluctant grin. "It's time, sweetcakes, let's take it home."

Yeah, it was time, she'd done what she'd wanted. She'd proved to herself that there was more to life than fear. That she could indeed put it all on the line and take a risk.

But now there was a man down below, waiting for her, and he was the biggest risk of all. One she wanted with all her heart and could never have.

"Let's go," she said, determined not to let anything ruin her happiness.

She waited until Steve landed. "Oh, I can park it!" she cried.

"No, I think—"

"Please? Let me have my crowning glory." With careful concentration she followed Steve's terse directions and pulled straight in, toward the hangar and its opened doors. The small figures standing there gradually came into focus. One by one she made out each of the mechanics. Then Matt. Even

Holly. She saw Bryan, standing in the open hangar door, his pilot's uniform gracing his tall, leanly muscled body. He looked right at her, and though not one of his muscles seemed to relax, she would have sworn his eyes filled with relief.

Cocky now, she waved to him.

"Katie!" Steve yelled. "Keep both hands on the—"

Too late.

On the slight incline, the plane veered to the right. Three mechanics dove out of her way. Matt stood there a moment longer, his mouth hanging open in disbelief, terror in his eyes, before Holly tackled him and pulled him down to safety.

"Katie!"

"Steve, stop hollering, you're distracting me."

"But—"

"Hush!"

He only groaned and ducked.

She whizzed by without killing anyone.

That was her last thought as the plane's wing clipped the steel hangar side wall, buckling it like a cheap toy as the plane skidded to an abrupt halt ten feet short of her tie-down spot.

When the plane shuddered still, Katie opened her eyes and risked a peek at Steve.

He straightened, looked out the window and grimaced. "Hey, remember last week when you almost killed our vice president and you didn't get fired?"

"Yeah?"

"Hope your luck is still holding."

13

HEART IN HIS THROAT, Bryan hauled Katie out of the plane. Before her toes could even touch the ground he had her buried in his arms and he was never going to let her go.

Never.

It shocked him, scared the hell out of him, but he could no longer deny the truth.

He loved her.

Because his legs were weak, he pressed his back against the other side of the hangar, the good side, on the steel wall that wasn't buckled like a tin can, and sank to the ground with her in his lap.

"You're shaking," he whispered.

"No, that's you," Katie whispered back, holding him tighter. "Bryan…"

"No." Fear and anguish and panic all rolled together into temper that overcame him now that he was sitting. "What the hell was that, Katie? What got into you?"

"Well, I—"

"What were you doing up there taking a flying lesson, and from someone *else?*"

"It's—"

"Dammit, how could you risk yourself that way, in a plane that isn't mine, and then that—that *approach,* though I use the term loosely! What the hell was *that?*"

"My life is my own, Bryan."

"Yes, but I want in."

"You...want in. My life?"

"I meant it," he whispered. "I meant what I said in the hangar. I didn't realize it, God who would have thought, but Katie, it's true. I love you. Enough to give up stunting, enough to know that I'll never want another woman, enough to promise forever. But please, *please* don't ever fly again."

He shouldn't have asked it of her, he had no right to ask anything of her when she hadn't asked anything of him. Misery and regret washed over him. "Wait. That didn't come out right."

"You don't want me to ever fly again," she repeated slowly. "Interesting."

"Katie—"

"Whoops," she said, covering his mouth again when he would have spoken. "Still my turn." Ignoring the commotion around them as everyone picked themselves up and took inventory of the damage, she looked deep into his eyes. "I thought I wanted safety. Security. Stability."

"The three *S*'s," Holly said with disgust, dusting herself off. *"Boring."*

Katie ignored both her and the baleful glance Matt shot her as he wiped at his filthy trousers. She looked only at Bryan. "I wanted everything I never got from my father as a child."

When he softened with remorse, when his hands slid over her arms in a caress, she shook her head sharply and kept her hands firmly on his mouth. "Please. Let me say this, I have to get it out. I thought I wanted *safe* love. The quiet, reserved kind that isn't really love at all, but just a teaser for it." She sighed and smiled into his eyes. "I was wrong, Bryan, that's not what I want at all. I want true, heart-pounding, butterflies-in-the-stomach, *real* love."

He pulled her fingers away from his mouth. "I can't tell you how glad I am to hear that. But dammit, you risked your life today!"

"Exactly." She grinned at him proudly. "So now I know I'm capable of taking a risk. I know I can do this."

"Do…what exactly?" Damn, was he always going to be clueless around her?

"Silly man. Now I know I can love you." She

cupped his face and kissed him softly, so very softly his heart caught.

"You...love me."

"Yeah." Her eyes filled. "I tried to save the best for last."

"Katie, sweetheart, do me a little favor." He could hardly speak. "Say it again."

"I saved the best for last."

"The other," he said as patiently as he could. *"Repeat the other."*

Her eyes filled. One tear spilled over and as he gently swiped it away with his thumb, she said the words he'd been dying to hear.

"I love you, Bryan Morgan, with all my heart. Will you be mine? Forever?"

His own eyes stung, his throat burned. "That's supposed to be my line."

"Well then, say it already."

Another tear spilled over his fingers and he had no idea now which of them it belonged to. "Will you be mine, Katie Wilkins? Forever and ever?"

"I will," she promised, and they sealed the vow with a kiss.

"I guess your Christmas curse is over," Holly said behind them.

Julie was also there, and she smiled. "From this point on, she's Christmas blessed."

Around them the rest of the staff gathered oohing and aahing over Katie's erratic—and expensive—parking job.

Katie looked deeply and lovingly into Bryan's eyes. "Next time, I promise to let *you* teach me to fly, in *your* airplane. Okay?"

He gazed into her beautiful eyes as he stroked her cheek. Behind them he could see the damage to the hangar, the torn wing on the airplane and quickly calculated the expenses. He thought lovingly of his own planes, and how much they were worth. Behind her back he crossed his own fingers. "Next time," he said, and kissed her.

Modern Romance™
...seduction and
passion guaranteed

Tender Romance™
...love affairs that
last a lifetime

Sensual Romance™
...sassy, sexy and
seductive

Blaze
...sultry days and
steamy nights

Medical Romance™
...medical drama on
the pulse

Historical Romance™
...rich, vivid and
passionate

27 new titles every month.

*With all kinds of Romance for
every kind of mood...*

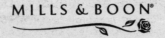

MILLS & BOON®

MB1

MILLS & BOON

CHRISTMAS SECRETS

Three Festive Romances

CAROLE MORTIMER   CATHERINE SPENCER
DIANA HAMILTON

Available from 15th November 2002

1202/59/MB50

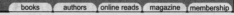

FREE

2 BOOKS
AND A SURPRISE GIFT!

We would like to take this opportunity to thank you for reading this Mills & Boon® book by offering you the chance to take TWO more specially selected titles from the Modern Romance™ series absolutely FREE! We're also making this offer to introduce you to the benefits of the Reader Service™—

★ FREE home delivery
★ FREE monthly Newsletter
★ FREE gifts and competitions
★ Exclusive Reader Service discount
★ Books available before they're in the shops

Accepting these FREE books and gift places you under no obligation to buy; you may cancel at any time, even after receiving your free shipment. Simply complete your details below and return the entire page to the address below. *You don't even need a stamp!*

YES! Please send me 2 free Modern Romance™ books and a surprise gift. I understand that unless you hear from me, I will receive 4 superb new titles every month for just £2.55 each, postage and packing free. I am under no obligation to purchase any books and may cancel my subscription at any time. The free books and gift will be mine to keep in any case.

P2ZEC

Ms/Mrs/Miss/Mr ....Initials ....
BLOCK CAPITALS PLEASE

Surname ....

Address ....

....

....Postcode ....

Send this whole page to:
UK: FREEPOST CN81, Croydon, CR9 3WZ
EIRE: PO Box 4546, Kilcock, County Kildare (stamp required)

Offer valid in UK and Eire only and not available to current Reader Service subscribers to this series. We reserve the right to refuse an application and applicants must be aged 18 years or over. Only one application per household. Terms and prices subject to change without notice. Offer expires 31st March 2003. As a result of this application, you may receive offers from Harlequin Mills & Boon and other carefully selected companies. If you would prefer not to share in this opportunity please write to The Data Manager at the address above.

Mills & Boon® is a registered trademark owned by Harlequin Mills & Boon Limited.
Modern Romance™ is being used as a trademark.